BOOK TWO

OF

THE FIGHTING TOMCATS

DIVIDED WE STAND

M. L. MAKI

Rose Hill Press, Olympia, Washington

Divided We Stand

Book Two of the Fighting Tomcat Series

First Edition

Cover design by Megan L. Maki

ACKNOWLEDGEMENTS

We would like to thank everyone who contributed advice or help on this project. Without your kind help, it would never have happened. Our family cheering section kept up our spirits when it got tough. We especially want to thank our beta readers, especially Michael Mohr, Robert Maki, Penny Sevedge. Our beta reader and assistant editor, Scott Richardson, just made Chief. Congratulations, Scott, you advice, insight, and support made this all possible.

DEDICATION

To our Beta readers:

ETNC (SW) Scott M. Richardson, Michael S. Mohr,
Robert Maki, and Penny Sevedge.

Thank you

The Fighting Tomcats

Book One

Fighting Her Father's War

Lieutenant Samantha 'Spike' Hunt thought she knew what she was getting into when she transferred from flying E-2C Hawkeye radar planes into the F-14 Tomcat fighters of the VF-154 Black Knights. She was planning her career to lead to astronaut training, but she found not all her fellow aviators were interested in sharing the squadron with women. Her Executive Officer, LCDR John 'Book' Carleton, undermined her anyway he could.

Then a lightning storm caused by a British experiment performed in the Australian desert caused her aircraft carrier, the USS Carl Vinson, and her battlegroup, to travel back in time from December, 1990 to December, 1941. Admiral Ren and Captain Johnson formed a brain trust, led by Reactor Officer, Captain Klindt and an assembled team of experts, including Lt. Hunt, to find out what just happened.

After an attack by a Japanese submarine sank the destroyer, USS Benjamin Stoddert, and they were able to piece together enough information, the brain trust determined they had come back in time to December, 1941, a few days after the attack on Pearl Harbor. Admiral

Ren, and the commanding officers of the remaining battlegroup, decided it was time to join the war, and they launched an 'alpha strike' to hit the Japanese who were invading the Philippines. In a day of fighting, they destroyed hundreds of Japanese aircraft, many transports, destroyers, cruisers, and one aircraft carrier, and saved their own battlegroup from a direct attack by the Japanese. Lt. Hunt racked up twenty-two aerial victories in the two engagements.

Her success angered Carleton, resulting in a confrontation between him and her flight leader, Lt. Stephan 'Swede' Swedenborg. Carleton is busted to Lieutenant and Lt. Hunt became the XO of the squadron.

It was a difficult time for the crews of the battlegroup, who are struggling with the loss of their families, their homes, and their place in time. Most of the people they love have not yet been born. So, they had a somber Christmas as they withdrew to report to Admiral Nimitz.

When they made contact with Admiral Nimitz, it does not take him long to understand the value of the ships, their equipment, and their people. He sends Admiral Ren, Captain Klindt, the CAG, Captain Lee, and other key people to Washington DC to reverse engineer the 1990's technology. The squadron leader of the Black Knights, Commander James 'Papa' Holtz is promoted to captain and becomes the CAG. Lt. Hunt is promoted by Admiral Nimitz to Lt. Commander and the command of the squadron.

Nimitz sends the battlegroup, under the command of Admiral Halsey on a Doolittle-like raid over Tokyo. Carleton's hate and anger escalates to the point he attempts to rape Lt. Hunt, but was interrupted by Chief White, whom he killed. But, just like the Doolittle raid, the battlegroup was discovered by a Japanese picket boat and they had to launch early. Carleton escaped from custody and joined the air battle.

In the attack over Tokyo, they discovered that a Japanese military airfield also had come back in time. They were successful in their raid on Tokyo, but the Japanese sent a missile counter-strike against the battle group. The sailors from the combined fleet found themselves fighting for their lives off the coast of Japan.

During the engagement to take out the Japanese F-15's that had attacked the battle group, Carleton attacked Hunt's plane. In the blue on blue furball, he forgot the enemy they were fighting and was shot down by a Japanese fighter.

When the squadrons returned to the fleet, it is on fire, and seven American ships have been hit.

LCDR Samantha Leigh Hunt, of Stone Mountain, Tennessee is fighting her father's war.

CONTENTS

Copyright

Acknowledgements

Dedication

Summary of Fighting Her Father's War, Book One of the Fighting Tomcats

Contents

Epigraph

Chapter 1

Chapter 2

Chapter 3

Chapter 4

Chapter 5

Chapter 6

Chapter 7

Chapter 8

Chapter 9

Chapter 10

Chapter 11

Chapter 12

Chapter 13

Chapter 14

Chapter 15

Chapter 16

Chapter 17

Chapter 18

Chapter 19

Chapter 20

Chapter 21

Chapter 22

Chapter 23

Notes

Glossary

About the Authors

One's mind, once stretched by a new idea, never regains its original dimensions.

Oliver Wendell Holmes

CHAPTER 1

BLACK KNIGHTS READY ROOM, 03 LEVEL, USS CARL VINSON

600 MILES SOUTH OF TOKYO

1604, 14 January, 1942

LCDR Samantha 'Spike' Hunt is exhausted. Fighting her fatigue, she struggles to formulate a plan to counter another air strike by the Japanese. After hitting Tokyo Bay with an alpha strike, the remaining F-14's ambushed F-15's that had come back on a Japanese air base. The ambush was successful, but the Japanese had mounted a major attack on the battlegroup. The squadrons come back to a damaged Carl Vinson, sinking cruisers and destroyers, and the loss of too many of their own.

"Swede, we have enough planes. You…" Her head drops and she stiffens, shaking her head and squeezing her eyes tight, "You, Hot Pants, Glow Rod, and Jedi man up a flight and report ready."

"Spike, you're exhausted. Let me handle, it. Okay?"

"I'm not going to fly, Swede. I know I can't, but the Japanese could counterstrike any time. Go."

"Yes, ma'am."

Spike turns to her RIO, "Puck, more coffee, please." Lt. JG Eric 'Puck' Hawke, a Lakota Sioux, grabs her cup, fills it, and sets it by her hand.

"Here. You know Swede is right. You're wiped out. Even Pappa told you to go to bed when he left."

"Okay, Puck. I'll go. Just keep things running here. We have seven operational birds and four on ready five. The Tomcatters assume ready five in about 40 minutes. Wake me up if anyone gets hurt, or any additional birds need to be taken out of…"

Admiral Halsey walks in and Cooper, her Yeoman, says, "Attention on deck."

They all stand and Spike finishes, "…of the lineup. Sir?"

"Are you alright, Commander?"

"I'll live, sir."

"I know what happened between you and Lt. Carleton."

"Yes, sir."

"It was exactly what I was afraid of when I heard of female sailors. Are you going to be able to continue?"

"I thought you would be more worried that we might die. I've got it, sir."

"Good." Then he turns and walks from the room.

GERMAN MiG-29A, 150 FEET ABOVE THE ENGLISH CHANNEL

Captain Henrik Getz scans the skies and his instruments as his aircraft approaches England. He is cruising along at full military power, just below the speed of sound. When he sees the white cliffs, he climbs to clear them, checking that his wingman is doing the same.

Getz scans the skies, then his instruments, as his aircraft approaches England. He muses over the last months of training Germans to fly jets He is still amazed. Time travel? How could it be? But, still, today he will get to attack the enemies of his country, East Germany. Yes, Germany was united again. In truth, at this time his beloved Germany has never been separated.

As the countryside flashes by only 200 feet below him, he knows he is on target. At the correct moment, he rolls his plane to the left and pulls into a smooth turn. As he does, he sees the roofs of Canterbury below him. It won't be long.

LONG BEACH, 02 LEVEL, FORWARD SUPERSTRUCTURE

1712, 14 January, 1942

MM1 Walters leads a hose team he's managed to cobble together. He is on his second OBA canister when he makes it up the port ladder. On the O2 level the fire is everywhere. The water boils when it hits the bulkheads and decks. He has another team trying to keep his team cool with low velocity fog. In places, the aluminum structure is burning, blue flames flaring out. When he sprays the aluminum bulkhead, the water flashes to steam. He turns his head and shouts down the line, "Send for PKP!"

He continues trying to knock down the flames, but they just relight as he does. Then the forward bulkhead begins a slow collapse. MM3 Small arrives with a hand-held PKP extinguisher and sprays the bulkhead. For a moment, the fire goes out. It relights quickly, but now the water can start cooling the metal. They spray the PKP every few seconds to keep the flames down, then hose down the bulkheads to cool them. In time, a very long time, the aluminum is too cold to support combustion and the fire goes out.

BLACK KNIGHTS READY ROOM

1715, 14 January

Spike stands, "Okay, Puck. Keep me posted. I'm going to bed."

"Do you need help getting to your stateroom?"

She shakes her head, "I got it." Then stumbles. She looks up at Puck and grins, as he offers a hand, "You'd think I'd had a few too many. Damn. I'll be fine."

"Spike, it's okay to ask for help."

"I know, but I need you here." She makes her way out of the ready room. The movement of the carrier through the light seas is enough to force her to put a hand on the bulkhead to steady herself. Turning, she walks into the stateroom she shares with Gloria. Grabbing her shower bag, she goes to the head. As she holds down the button to get wet, the tears come in wrenching sobs.

If I wasn't so damn tired. If I could just stop seeing Chief White's face. If. If. If. I'll get through this. I will. I can do it. So much death.

CHAPTER 2

USS SAN FRANCISCO, BRIDGE

1732, 14 January, 1942

Captain Cassin Young is still on the bridge wing. His steward puts a cup of coffee and a sandwich in his captain's hands, hoping he'll eat. LCDR Valentine Carmichael, the Damage Control Assistant, approaches and salutes. Captain Young returns the salute with his coffee cup, "How bad?"

"Sir, we have two dead, seven wounded, fires out. We lost mount 54. It's mangled and will need yard repairs. The turret barbette held. It's dented, but that's all."

"That's good news. Mount 2 still functional, then?"

"Yes, sir, fully functional."

"Thank you. I need to send this to Halsey. I need the list of the dead and wounded." Carmichael hands him the list, "Good job, Commander. See about sending anyone we can to the Long Beach and the Salt Lake City."

"Yes, sir." He salutes and leaves.

EIGHTBALLER 4, ABOVE USS FANNING SURVIVORS

0134, 15 January, 1942

Sandra "Cargo Britches" Douglas hovers thirty feet above the waves as another load of sailors is hoisted aboard. Her SEALs, HM1 Larry 'Munchkin' Shockley and ENS Russel 'Triage' Jeremy, are gathering the swimming sailors and trying to keep the sharks at bay. Out of her lower windshield she sees one of the SEALs diving under the water. A moment later a shark is thrashing the water and there is blood everywhere.

Soon her bird is full and the two crazy frogmen are hoisted aboard. Munchkin is holding something under his t-shirt and the two are doing a high five on the way up.

Once aboard, and the sailors are tended to, Triage puts on a crew helmet. "Lieutenant, we have three critical. One is a bad bleeder and the others have multiple compound fractures."

"Understood, we are heading for Vinson. What's under Shockley's shirt?"

"Shark steak. He figured if he had to kill it, we might as well get some grub out of it."

CAPTAIN HENRIK GETZ'S MiG-29 APPROACHING LONDON

Getz is thrilled as he sees the roof tops of London appear ahead of him. He's flying at just below Mach 1, so he knows his approach is silent. For nine years of flying for the East German Airforce, he dreamt of this day. When unification happened, he was thrilled for his people, but sad, as it meant East Germany had lost. The Soviet Union collapsed. It was like losing the world cup without ever playing a game.

His squadron was assigned to Brendenmeyer Air Base to train NATO pilots. Then whole thing went back in time to World War II. At least now, he would get to fight. He would prove himself to be the best. Most of his peers refused to fight and were imprisoned. Insanity.

Adjusting west in a shallow curve, he levels his wings and lines up on a fuel tank and pickles off a 500-pound bomb. As he circles back, the flak makes it harder to see the streets below him. His next target was maddeningly small and hard to find, which was the point. Missing it the first time, he circles and tries again. As he does, he sees a warship in the Docklands area and drops a 500-pound bomb on it. Then he recognizes the street he's looking for, lines up, and drops a 500 pounder on the corner of the Treasury building, hitting what is supposed to be the War Cabinet Rooms.

Now he turns his attention to the Spitfires and Hurricanes his wingman was dealing with, quickly downing two fighters. Calling on the radio, he says, "Herman, we go home."

ON THE TOWER BRIDGE, LONDON

Prime Minister Winston Churchill climbs from his hastily stopped Bentley and looks off to the east as the jets wing away. Rolling a cigar between his fingers in thought he climbs back into the car, "Take me to the Treasury building."

As they pull up, he can see the fire brigade working. "Yes, right. William take me to Downing."

03 LEVEL FORWARD SUPERSTRUCTURE, USS LONG BEACH

0150, 15 January, 1942

Walters continues through the melting structure to the 03 level and repeats the process. By the time he makes it to the 05 level, the only thing burning is normal combustibles. Three hours and eight OBA canisters later, the fire is out.

When Walters takes off his face mask, the stench of burning plastic, wood, metal, and flesh hits him. Handing his hose to one of his team, he grabs a rake, digging through the mess looking for hotspots. The missile hit here, and it is here that the fire was hottest. He crouches down under the partially collapsed 03 level to rake out coals. With his back to the 03 level and his feet on the 02 level, he can feel movement between them. Stepping back out he sees Captain Tenzar.

"Careful, sir, it's not stable."

"Are you MM2 Walters?"

'Yes, sir."

"I understand it was you who called for the PKP."

"Yes, sir, it seemed reasonable at the time."

Tenzar laughs, "It was brilliant. I've never heard of anyone putting out an aluminum fire."

"Thank you, sir."

"No, son, thank you. How are we doing here?"

"Sir, we need to do something about the box. If we're caught in a storm it could break off. I can feel it move now."

Tenzar puts a hand on the overhead feeling the slight movement, "I see what you mean. Any ideas?"

"I was thinking, sir, if we punched holes along the 02 and 03 floor beams and wove a cable through them, we could use a chain fall to tighten it up and then clamp it in place."

"Uh. You propose to sew the ship together? Why not weld it in place?"

"Sir, it's moving. The welds would break as we made them."

"Good point. I'll talk to the DCA. You go and get some rest. Thank you, again."

BRIDGE, USS SALT LAKE CITY

0216, 15 January, 1942

LCDR Brewster Flanagan, the CHENG, walks up to Captain Zacharias, his uniform soaking wet and covered in oil and grime. Saluting, he says, "Fires are out, overhaul is in progress. Fire main is restored aft of mount 2. Mount 2 is flooded. The bulkhead between mount 2 and the store room is sprung. We have five submersibles going, but we are losing the battle. The forward bulkhead to fire room 1 is leaking, but I'm hoping we can hold it there. If we do, we should be able to limp back for repairs."

"If we lose the fire room, what then?"

"Sir, if we lose the fire room, we lose the ship."

"What do you need?"

Flanagan shrugs, "More pumps, more shoring, more people that know how to use it. Maybe a couple of cutting torches to remove debris."

"I'll get them for you. You are doing wonders, Brewster. Please give your men my thanks."

Flanagan salutes, "Aye sir, I will." He looks out over the battle group, "I see the fires on Long Beach are out. Good." Turning, he heads back below.

FLIGHT DECK CONTROL, USS FIFE

0421, 15 January, 1942

Lt. JG Laura Wakefield watches one of her helo's take off, and on radio, "Thank you, Easy Rider 31. Good day."

The phone talker beside her says, "Ma'am, BM1, um, the conning officer wants to order a backing bell."

She picks up the phone and hears, "The Long Beach is getting close. I need to go right rudder and back down."

She says, "Right full rudder, back full emergency."

The ship begins to shake as the Fife turns. When the turn slows because all the way is off, she says, "All stop. Conning officer, you cannot be tentative. The safety of the ship rides on you."

BM1 Coates says, "Ma'am, I've never done this."

"I've never been a captain, either. Boats, you're all I've got, so please get it together. The fires are out and we have shipped out the worst of our casualties. Keep us on station while I put together a report for Admiral Halsey. God, I never thought I'd say that."

10 DOWNING STREET, LONDON

Churchill, alone in his office, lights a cigar and picks up his phone, "Put me through to Roosevelt." A moment later his phone rings, "Franklin, I have a problem. It seems the

Krauts have also been blessed with future aircraft. They just laid an egg on my war room. Could you find a way to spare some of those naval aircraft you spoke of?"

Roosevelt replies, "Good God! You are certain?"

"I am. I saw them myself. High speed, no propeller, and they were very loud as they passed. There is no doubt."

"Indeed. The issue is rather simple. Impressive though they be, they are limited in range. Right now, they are off Japan, half the world away."

"I see. Well, my friend. Have you any idea how long before we may be reinforced?"

"I don't know, but I can find out."

"Please do. I am concerned that, should your Navy dither too long, they may not have an England to defend."

CHAPTER 3

RAIL ROAD YARD, NIZHNY, TAGIL, USSR

Colonel General Yuri Kryukov stands with his staff officer, Major General Grigory Stepanov, silently watches armored vehicles being loaded on rail cars. It is a huge operation that is being, carefully, but quickly done. Occasionally, one of the soldiers or workman glances at the tall man, impressive in his camouflage uniform. Hundreds of rail cars are needed to move just one of his divisions.

An aide approaches, salutes, and hands him a folder. Opening it, he reads quickly, signs the paper, and hands it back. As the solder leaves, he turns to Stepanov, "It is as we thought. He is in a dacha near Gzhel."

"It couldn't be better. Gzhel is on the railroad."

Yuri nods, allowing himself a brief smile. "Yes. It is good."

NUMBER 1 FIRE ROOM, USS SALT LAKE CITY

0630, 15 January, 1942

There are so many fire hoses down the hatches of number 1 fire room that Captain Zacharias has to squeeze between them to go below. He can feel the ship settling down at the bow, and estimates it at about 10 degrees. Working his way down between the four large boilers to mid-level, he finds LCDR Flanagan studying a drawing, "How is it?"

The CHENG looks up, "We're still fighting. We've isolated the eductor system at the forward bulkhead, but that has sprung near the top of lower level. As the level climbed in the store rooms forward, it increased the pressure here. We're trying to shore below and pack in the cracks."

"Can you stop the water here?"

"We're trying, sir. The fuel bottoms here are now contaminated with sea water. I was just figuring out how we can fill the day tanks from back aft."

"I understand, but there's another problem. We need to get the fleet moving. We're backing right now at one third, but we are still in range of additional attacks and two of the missile ships are disabled. Could this bulkhead take the pressure of a forward bell?'

A look of deep misery passes over Flanagan's face, "I don't know, sir. I would like more shoring before we try."

SAMANTHA'S AND GLORIA'S STATEROOM

0640, 15 January, 1942

Sam wakes with a start. Her mouth feels like an old wool sock, her head fuzzy and pounding. Trying to sit up, she realizes she's in the bottom bunk. Hearing movement above her, she croaks out, "Gloria."

Gloria pops her head over the side, "So, like Lazarus, the dead are alive. I'll get you some water." Climbing down, she gets a water and hands it to Sam. Sam drinks, coughs, then finishes the bottle, feeling her flesh soak it in.

"What's the time, and what the hell happened?"

"0640, and you tell me. When I got back from ready five, your shower bag was on the floor and you were collapsed on my bed. Fluffy took it on himself to guard our stateroom all night. Puck wouldn't tell me what's going on, so give."

"Can I have another bottle of water, please?"

Gloria, sitting on a chair, hands her an open bottle. Sam, swings her legs off the bed and chugs it. She wipes her mouth, looking at the floor. "Carleton tried to rape me." She looks up and they exchange a silent look, "Chief White tried to save me. Carleton knifed him. He's dead." She feels herself tearing up and wipes them away, annoyed. Gloria hands her some tissues, "I managed to get control and hold him until the MAA showed up, then I flew the mission to Tokyo."

"Oh, my God, Sam!"

"Carleton tried to kill us out there. He tried to shoot us down. The Japanese got a missile into him instead." She finishes the second bottle.

"Okay, damn. Okay. Are you up to wardroom 3 for coffee and breakfast?"

"Yeah, I think I can make it. Coffee, oh yeah, and Gloria?"

"Yes, honey."

"Thank you."

"You're welcome, but Puck's the one you really have to thank. I didn't carry you all over the ship."

They get dressed in flight suits and leave their stateroom. Fluffy is still standing there with a tire iron is his hand. "Morning ladies. You look a good bit better this morning, Skipper."

"Thank you, Fluffy. Have you been up all night?"

"I was spelled for a bit, ma'am. Shall I tell Swede and Puck that you're up?"

"Yes, we'll be in wardroom 3, and thank you, again."

In wardroom 3, Sam gets a full breakfast, coffee, and more water. She's still damn thirsty. As she's sitting down with Gloria, Puck and Swede come in and sit across from them. Swede asks, "You okay, boss?"

"Better, thank you." Looking at Puck, "Thanks so much. Are you okay?"

Eric smiles, "Yeah, just another interesting day at war. Halsey, Johnson, and Holtz want to talk to you."

Sam grins, "That can wait for now. They have my report from last night. Swede where does the squadron stand?"

"We have nine birds serviceable, with 733 being the current hangar queen. Glow Rod over G'd the hell out of his bird, so it's going to be down awhile. We've been cannibalizing it to keep the others flying. The admiral and captain are out surveying the damage, so you have some time. As you know, there was no second strike. Nimitz cancelled it. Jedi and Gunner are on ready 5, and the Tomcatters have the CAP. BUG and Joker are still out there. With the damage to the fleet, they haven't been able to spare too many helos for fishing out flyers.

"Hopefully, someone finds them. Packs wants to see you. Carleton is dead. He landed in the water with a broken neck. At least, that's what the corpsman says."

"Thank you, Stephan."

WAR DEPARTMENT, WASHINGTON, DC

1530 local time, 15 January, 1942

Admiral King walks into the conference room, followed by Admirals Ren and Lee, and without preamble says, "Well, George, what is the crisis today?

General George Marshall replies, "We need to move some of your fighter jets to England. The Germans seem to have their own jet fighters."

Admiral Ren, "They are off Japan with some damage. It's going to take a while to get the Vinson to England."

Marshall replies, "Our friends do not need the Vinson. They need the fighters. How long to ferry them to England?"

King asks, "How many planes do the Germans have?"

Marshall says, "We don't know. The initial attack involved two."

Lee says, "I don't believe most German pilots would willingly fight for Hitler. He is despised."

King says, "Perhaps it is Germans from our time flying the aircraft?"

Ren says, "No, sir. They haven't had near enough time to train. These have to be from 1990."

Brigadier General Walter Altman says, "They can't be that hard to fly. I'm a pilot. A plane is a plane."

Lee looks at him, "Have you ever flown at one thousand six hundred knots? These aircraft perform at a whole different level. The engines require specific management skills. The avionics are very different. It would take a year at minimum to train new pilots. Something else to think of, we had U.S. and British aircraft co-located at many NATO fields. There could be captured servicemen and women and their families in Germany."

Altman looks at him, incredulous, "That's idiotic! Why would you do that?"

Lee says, "We won the war. Afterward we needed Germany as a bulwark against Russia. Don't judge a time period you know nothing about."

Altman, persisting, "But they are our enemy."

Lee says, "So was England, once. Things change. Anyway, they are probably there."

Marshall says, "On task, gentlemen. How do we get the aircraft to England?"

Ren says, "We sail her through the Suez via Australia."

Altman says, "We sail your carrier to the Bremerton Yard as planned, then ferry them across the country from field to field. As I understand, they can safely land at a bomber base."

Lee says, "True, but we would have to ferry out about 60,000 gallons of jet fuel, parts for possible problems, and ground crew to every stop. The fighters will outstrip the transports carrying everything, making it a logistic nightmare. What do we do if the field maintenance people do not take FOD seriously, and we grenade an engine? No, it's better to ferry them via ship."

King asks, "Could we load them on another ship and ferry them that way?"

Ren says, "Maybe. Do you have a carrier that can handle the weight on their deck? Each F-14 weighs 48,000 pounds dry."

King shakes his head, "No, it will have to be the Vinson. How do we do it?"

CHAPTER 4

FLIGHT DECK, SPOT 2, USS CARL VINSON

0800, 15 January, 1942

Halsey and Johnson walk toward an SH-3. Two F-14s are parked at ready 5, and a Red Cock F-18 is launching from cat 3. As the noise drops, Halsey asks, "Do you know this Commander Grey?"

"No, sir, but Captain Tucker and Captain Tenzar both give him high marks."

"I want to meet him first. I understand he was uninjured when he escaped off the bridge of the Long Beach."

They climb aboard, put on their helmets, and plug into the communications system, "Yes, sir, just a bump on the head. They plucked him and the bridge crew off the signal bridge by helicopter and landed them on the fan tail. There were some minor injuries, but Commander Grey is fine."

Halsey asks, "Who is flying this contraption?"

"I am, sir. LCDR David Crocker, sir, commander of the Eightballers."

"Commander, I want to take a run around the fleet, then land briefly on the Long Beach. From there it's straight to the Horne. Do we have the fuel?"

"Yes, sir, no problem. We'll hot pump on the Long Beach to top off."

"Can she spare the fuel?"

Johnson says, "Sir, the Long Beach is nuclear powered. She keeps aviation fuel for her diesels and for fueling helicopters."

Halsey says, "I still don't understand all this atom hocus pocus. Oh, my Lord!" They are flying across the front of the Salt Lake City. She's down at the bow to the point that the main deck is nearly awash.

Johnson says, "It's amazing she's still afloat."

"They are fighting her and I'm loath to cut her loose or scuttle her. If we steam off and leave her, she'll be sunk for sure. If we stick with her, we're all in jeopardy."

Then they pass the Fife. There's still smoke coming from the gaping hole left by the lost superstructure. As they get closer, they can see the hole reaches all the way to the second deck. Halsey asks, "This ship, it's the one that lost all of its senior officers. It's being commanded by a female lieutenant junior grade, correct?"

"Yes, sir, Lt. JG Laura Wakefield. She has damage control well in hand. She transferred the bridge to the helicopter control booth in the aft of the ship because it's the only place with a radio. They have propulsion, weapons on line, and are trying to put together a temporary bridge. We have a crew on board helping clear debris."

"Do you know her?"

"Not really, sir. I met her once briefly. She seemed bright and cheerful, but it's only a first impression."

Then they circle the Long Beach. It's clear the box superstructure is leaning forward, and they can see the crew weaving cable through it, trying to hold it in place. Halsey says, "Damn, it's a wonder she's still afloat."

"The problem is the superstructure, sir. To save weight they made it out of aluminum. After a missile hit, the aluminum burns."

"What an idiotic thing to do."

"Yes, sir."

"Let's set down, Commander. We'll be taking on a passenger, and then on to the Horne."

As they flare and land, Captain Tenzar and Commander Grey are standing between the tomahawk box launchers. Halsey asks, "What's in the boxes?"

"Tomahawk missiles, sir. Long range cruise missiles with a variety of warheads. The problem is they depend on a satellite system that we no longer have."

They step out of the helicopter, running out from under the blades, holding their hats. Tenzar and Grey salute as they approach. Saluting, Halsey asks, "What's the status of repairs, Captain?"

Tenzar replies, "We'll have the box locked down in about an hour. After that we're ready to go. Mount 2 is disabled, as is 3 and 4 directors. The 48 radar is down, but the 49 still works. Bridge steering is damaged, so we are steering from aft steering. We have full propulsion capability and fifty percent on weapons. Best we can do until we get to the yards."

Halsey says, "You've done an admirable job, Captain, as has your fine crew. I'm sorry to be stealing your XO, though."

"I understand the need, Admiral."

Halsey turns to Grey, "Might I have a word before we leave?"

Grey says, "Of course, sir," and they step away.

Halsey asks, "How long have you served, Commander?"

"Seventeen years."

"Where are you from?"

"A small town in Oregon, The Dalles, sir."

"College?"

"University of Washington, physics, sir."

"Alright, I want to explain my command philosophy. First, I expect you to think. I want you to solve problems and take care of your crew. They need to know you care. I believe the commander in the field knows better than I do what needs to be done. But I expect you to do it. Do you follow me?"

"Yes, sir."

"Next, I expect your vessel to be ready to sortie and fight at a moments notice. If you need to make repairs or have a casualty, I need to know immediately. Bad news is best served fresh. Your job is to prepare your subordinates for command. Any captain who rules his wardroom like a tyrant is useless to me."

"Yes, sir."

"When it comes to fighting, I want to have to hold you back, not push you forward. Our country is paying us to kill Japs and by God, that is what we will do. Do you have any questions?'

"Sir, with the Long Beach damaged, the Horne has the best radar suite in the fleet. I think I should be AAW commander."

Halsey nods and smiles, "I'll look into that. Tenzar did a good job, but you have a point. Let's rejoin the others for you pinning. Oh, another thing, can I have your oak leaves after you're pinned?"

"Of course, sir."

Halsey and Grey walk back and Halsey hands Tenzar captains' eagles, "Captain Tenzar, would you please pin these on Commander Grey?" After that is done, Grey hands Halsey his oak leaves.
"Well, that's done. We have it to do. Thank you, Captain Tenzar." Tenzar salutes, and the three officers turn to go, Grey carrying his bags. Halsey says to Grey as they lift off, "So, Captain, you know what to expect?"

"I think so, sir."

"You're right, with the Long Beach disabled, you are the AAW commander."

"Yes, sir, thank you for your confidence in me."

"Sir, Captain Tucker and Captain Tenzar speak highly of you, and it is on their judgment I do this. Do live up to their expectations, sir."

"Yes, sir."

In a few minutes, Eightballer 1 is settling on the flight deck of the USS Horne. As they step off the bird, they hear, "Carrier Group 2 arriving, Carl Vinson arriving, Captain, United States Navy arriving." Captain Rodgers is waiting for them, with Commander Kettrick, his XO.

Walking up to Rodgers, Halsey hands him his orders. Rodgers reads them and pales. Halsey says, "I can't have my captains hiding behind defenseless ships while there is a fight on. Captain Rodgers, turn over to your replacement, sir."

Rodgers turns to Grey, and Grey salutes, "I relieve you, sir."

Rodgers returns the salute, "I stand relieved." He turns to Halsey, "I need to get my things."

"They will be sent for. Come with me."

Halsey, Johnson, and Rodgers board Eightballer 1. Halsey gets his crew helmet on and asks, "Commander Crocker, would it be a problem to land briefly on the Fife? I want to meet her captain."

"No, sir, not at all." He calls to inform Fife, and in a few minutes, they are on the helicopter pad.

Halsey looks at Rodgers, "Stay on the helicopter, Captain Rodgers. We'll only be a minute."

Halsey and Johnson step out of the bird, running to clear the blades, and holding their hats. Saluting them is a short athletic woman, curly blonde hair in a tight bun. She wipes a curl off her face as the 1MC announces, "Carrier Group 2 arriving, Carl Vinson arriving."

Rodgers watches as the two men return her salute. Halsey says, "You're doing a fine job, Lieutenant Wakefield. Do you have full propulsion back yet?"

"Yes, sir. We've patched the damage to our forward stack. We're still trying to throw together a bridge. Conning from here is impossible."

"What do you need?"

"A shipyard would be nice, but a couple of welders and some plate will do. I need to cut away the mast and stow it clear of the Mark 41. I may need to come alongside and use the Vinson's AB crane for that. I also need to put together a bridge forward of the funnel. I already have electricians and ET's running the wire. I would like a bit of a roof over it, though."

"You lost a lot of crew. We have some people available, but they've never served on a ship like this."

"That would be fine, sir. We can train them. Sir, who are you going to put in charge."

"How long have you been in the Navy, Lieutenant?"

"Seven years, sir."

"A long time for a JG."

"I'm a mustang, sir. I served as a nuclear field machinist mate before being selected for OCS."

"Been to college?"

"Yes, sir. BS in mechanical engineering from San Diego State University."

"Do you know how to navigate? I mean, with a sextant?"

"Yes, sir, of course."

"What is the primary mission of this vessel, Lieutenant?"

"To protect the carrier, sir. The Fife is primarily anti-submarine, but as you've seen, we have some anti-air."

"Who is the youngest person on your ship?"

"Seaman Megan Lockwood, sir. She just turned eighteen."

"You ask me who is going to be in charge, Lieutenant. The answer is, you are. Please remove your collar devices."

"Yes, sir?" reaching up to remove her lieutenant junior grade silver bars.

Halsey steps forward and pins Commander Grey's oak leaves to her collar. "A command like this needs the rank of commander. Congratulations, Commander," and shakes her hand.

Startled, Commander Laura Wakefield salutes Halsey, "I will do my best, sir."

He returns her salute, "You already are."

Rodgers watches this in stunned silence. Then Halsey and Johnson return to the helo. On the way back to Vinson, Halsey says, "Captain, I really enjoyed that. I have more than a few misgivings about females in service, but after what she's done to save her ship, I feel she deserves her shot. Besides, we don't have a lot of men who know how that ship works. She seems to be a competent leader. It's hers to lose." They are silent for the rest of the return flight to Vinson.

CHAPTER 5

OUTSIDE BLACK KNIGHT READY ROOM

0915, 15 January, 1942

Swede walks up to Spike, "I have a plan for an operation I wanted to show you."

"Okay."

"I need you take on it, because it's a little hare-brained."

"I have to talk to Packs first. Is he in the ready room?"

"He should be." He opens the door. When they walk in, the room is quiet. The television is off and no one is playing cards. Packs is alone on the far side of the room.

Thud runs up to her, "You're okay!" then stops. "I'm sorry, Spike. I'm sorry. Carleton got on your six. It's all my fault."

"No, Thud, it's not your fault. It's his."

Packs walks over, his arm in a sling and sporting a shiner. "Spike, I'm the one who's sorry. I couldn't get him to stop."

Spike nods her head, "Frank, can you give us a minute?" and walks Packs into her office and shuts the door. "Grab a chair, we need to talk."

He sits down, "Ma'am, there is so much I should have done. I mean, I knew he didn't like you. My God, I probably encouraged him."

"First of all, thank you for lighting us up so we knew you were back there."

"It's the only thing I could think to do. My radio was glitch…um, shit, he disabled it."

"Probably. Look, he just couldn't handle the transition back in time. It wrapped him up too tight. Packs, do you know if he was married or had kids?"

"Yeah, his kids and mine played together a lot, though our wives didn't get along."

"How old are, um, were your babies? I'm sorry. The time travel thing. That was rude."

"Jennifer is, was eleven, and Mary was ten."

"Why didn't Book's wife and yours get along, if I'm not being too nosy?"

"It's okay. Lorraine, well, she felt an officer's wife should focus on the kids, the house, and the community. When the squadron was out, Trisha would go out drinking and dancing. It wasn't a great marriage. Do you suppose that's why he didn't like women?"

"Could be."

"Crazy thing is, when we got home, she'd go all nuts on him and accuse him of cheating. As far as I know, he never did. I would have known."

"Thanks. So, how are you doing?"

"I won't lie. It's been hard. I have my faith to fall back on, but still. In a way, it's easier to know they don't exist, then if they had died."

"I can't imagine. I have my brother, and we're close, but it's not the same. But, yeah, it's easier that he doesn't exist. Sort of."

Looking down, "I've heard, ma'am. I know Chief…I know what he did to you and Chief White. I guess everyone knows."

"Lyle, it's okay. You couldn't have known. You did what you could and it's not your fault. Are we good?"

"Yeah, I'm a little banged up, but we're good." Packs smiles.

She chuckles, "I'm so glad. So now, we need to find you a new pilot. It's going to take time. We're going to need trainers, too"

"Ma'am, I've already been thinking about it. We've lost planes. They might find Bug and Joker. I know they're looking. The Tomcatters have also lost two birds. The thing is, the F-18 squadrons have lost four planes and have one more so beat up, it's doubtful it will ever fly again. Most of the pilots will probably be recovered because they ejected over water. So, maybe, we could transition one to fly in front of me."

"Good idea, a really good idea. I'll talk to their CO's and see what can be done. Do you have any other brilliant ideas? You're on a roll."

Packs gives her a wry smile, "No, ma'am. One a day is my limit."

"Okay, then, we've kept Swede waiting long enough. Let's go back." She puts out her hand, "Lyle, thank you," and he takes it.

Almost all the pilots and RIOs are in the ready room and all eyes follow her and Packs as they walk out. Spike drawls, smiling, "Come on guys, don't you all have some work to do?" They all look at each other and start laughing.

Swede motions to her, "Come look at the map, Spike. Papa's TARPS recon pod lost power when he took a couple of rounds from an F-4. We didn't get a very good picture of what happened. I've an idea for launching a recon mission." He explains his plan.

When he's done, Spike says, "It's kind of nuts, but it should work. I agree, we need to know what we bought for all our loses. I'll talk to higher. I will need to anyway."

Swede says, "Halsey and Johnson are still out touring the fleet."

"Okay, I would prefer to talk to them all at once, anyway. Could you ask ADC Gellar to meet me in the power plant shop?"

BLACK KNIGHTS POWER PLANT SHOP

1000, 15 January, 1942

When Spike walks into the shop, the whole division is there. She stops and surveys the room. AD1 McCrimmon is reading through paperwork. ADC Gellar is sitting in a chair looking a million miles away, and the rest of the crew are standing around, distracted and listless. Joe Cervella says, "Chief, Skipper's here."

Gellar's head shoots up and he briefly makes eye contact, then looks away, "I'm sorry, ma'am, Book beat up the Master at Arms and the doc, then ran off."

"Book is dead."

"Yeah, I know."

"It's his fault, not yours. You did everything you could."

"I just wished I figured it out sooner. I found the note. That's how he got you down here, isn't it?"

"Yes."

"Anyway, I brought it to the Chief. He figured it out."

"I see. I left the note on the bird."

"If I'd figured it out that it wasn't Chief's handwriting, I could have stopped him before…"

"NO! Then you would be dead. The first person to walk through that door was dead. That's just the way it was."

"Did you shoot him down, ma'am?"

"No, the Japanese did. While he was after us, he forgot they were out there."

Gellar nods and Lori asks, "Are you okay, ma'am? We all heard about Lt. Hawke carrying you all over the ship, and Fluffy grabbing the corpsman."

Spike laughs, "Yeah, I'm fine. I was just exhausted. Thanks, Lori."

Joe asks, "What are they gonna do? They can't arrest him. He's dead."

"I don't know. I'll be talking to the command about that later, but that isn't why I came down here. I came down to see if you're all okay."

Gellar says, "I feel better just talking to you, ma'am. Ma'am, yer gonna need a new chief now. Can I come back to the squadron?"

"Can your LPO with the Tomcatters hack it as a chief?"

"He's more ready than Socks, ma'am. Socks has been a first class only a few days."

"You're right. I'll look into it. You may have to look after both divisions until your LPO has got it."

"That's okay. Um, ma'am, is there any way we can have him buried with honors? You know, like he fought the enemy?"

"I'll talk to the command. That's a good idea. Where's Duck?"

"His friend was in our berthing 'cause they kicked him out of medical. The missile hit near there and he got hurt again putting out fires. He saved our berthing, ma'am. Anyway, Duck is looking after him in medical."

Spike laughs, "Thank you. I believe the Stoddert grew heroes."

FIRE ROOM 1, USS SALT LAKE CITY

1135, 15 January, 1942

The crew of the Salt Lake worked through the night and morning getting her ready to turn and make way forward, instead of aft. Backing at two thirds, they'd at least been able to keep the fleet moving. Two thirds, because after forty minutes of back full, the engines started to overheat, so a two thirds bell was all they could do. Captain Zacharias went down to the fire room to look over the situation. The shoring of the forward bulkhead is extensive. Most of the cracks have been filled with putty and cloth, then covered in wood, so the leaks have been significantly reduced. The portable pumps are secured as the installed eductor is keeping up. "Will she hold, Brewster?"

LCDR Flanagan says, "Sir, if it doesn't, there is nothing more I can do."

"Alright, Brewster, I'm going back up to turn us around. I'll step up the bells to standard. If we can do that, I feel it is good enough. Keep me informed."

"Yes, sir, I will." He watches Zacharias leave.

In a few minutes they hear the order for all stop, then ahead one third. Flanagan goes down to the lower level, telling the watch standers to move up to middle level. Then, he checks the bulkhead. Picking up a sound powered phone, "Bridge, Engineer, bulkhead is holding."

The order for two thirds is given. Flanagan again reports the bulkhead is holding. Then the order for ahead standard is given. As the ship comes up on the bell, she begins to shake. "Captain, we have some vibration here." As he is speaking, a wedge shoots out of a shoring piece and the shore slips violently, hitting a pump casing. "Sir, we're losing her!" The forward bulkhead starts to collapse inward and Flanagan grabs a piece of wood, attempting to brace the bulkhead.

Then section after section of the shoring gives way, and water pours in. Realizing it's lost, he pulls himself through the water to the ladder, but the current pushes him away.

He finds himself pushed against a deck grate on the starboard side of the fire room. As the salt water hits the boilers, it flashes to putrid smelling steam. He pushes against the deck grate, but the water keeps pushing him around. Then, BT1 Rivera sees him and starts frantically pulling on the grate. He struggles with the stuck grate and just as the water reaches Flanagan's head, the grate gives. Rivera pulls Flanagan up and out.

"Thank you, Charley. Did you pull the fires?"

"Yes, sir. I was doing it when I saw you."

"Charley, I believe it's time to leave. The old girl's a goner."

BRIDGE, USS CARL VINSON

1215, 15 January, 1942

Halsey watches the Salt Lake City slow to a stop. She's now awash to the forward stack, the bridge an island surrounded by water. He picks up the radio, "Captain Zacharias, she is lost. Chester, go alongside to take off the crew." The USS Chester, a Northampton class heavy cruiser moves into position by the Salt Lake City.

Captain Johnson on the 1MC, "Now launch all available helicopters to recover sailors off the Salt Lake City." All the helicopters of the task force launch into action, again.

A sailor walks onto the bridge, "Request to enter the bridge with a message."

The OOD looks over, "Enter."

The sailor walks up to Halsey with the message. Halsey signs for it, dismissing the sailor. He pulls out the message, reading it carefully. After a second time through, he hands the message to Johnson.

Johnson reads it, "Sydney Australia to affect repairs. Wonder what's up?"

"I don't know, Captain, but we need to make plans to split the fleet. I want to steam together until we are further away from Japan. If the Enterprise group gets caught by the Jap's without the Vinson around, they would be wiped out. I think Long Beach, Fife, and San Francisco need to go to Bremerton for repairs."

"I don't like the idea of being without the ASW that Fife offers."

"I see, Captain. We keep the Fife. But we need to get her a bridge. I'll schedule an all commander's call after the funeral service."

"Yes, sir."

SALT LAKE CITY BRIDGE

1225, 15 January, 1942

Captain Zacharias gives the order every captain dreads, "Salt Lake City, this is your Captain. All hands abandon ship. Chester is coming alongside, so keep it orderly. Officers, take charge of your men. All hands abandon ship."

The conning officer, Lt. Marker, asks, "Sir, will you be leaving?"

Zacharias waves him off, "Go, John. Tend to your division. They need you."

"We all need you, sir."

"You're right. Go. Get them ready. I'll see to the rest of the crew."

Some of the men end up in the water but are picked up quickly by boats from the Chester and Vinson and the helicopters. As the ship slips further into the water, Chester has to stand off. The last of the crew gather on the fan tail, where Captain Zacharias helps them into the helicopters. Soon, he is standing alone on the upturned stern.

Zacharias waves off a helicopter. Halsey grabs a bull horn and goes out on the weather deck, "Captain, I need you. Don't be foolish." The ship, only the stern exposed aft of mount 3, rolls upside down, throwing Zacharias into the water. Immediately, a SAR swimmer drops and the captain is plucked from the waves. As he's hoisted into the helo, the Salt Lake City slips beneath the water, bow first, to her grave 5600 feet below.

CHAPTER 6

OUTSIDE THE ADMIRAL'S PASSAGEWAY, USS CARL VINSON

1712, 15 January, 1942

LCDR Hunt, Lt. JG Hawke, and ADC Gellar wait. Lt. JG Lyle Boxter is in the Admiral's conference room giving his statement. After about twenty minutes, he steps out. "Puck, you're next." Puck smiles at Spike, puts a hand briefly on her shoulder, and walks in.

Packs looks at Spike, "That was hard, Spike, like re-living the whole thing."

"Yeah, I get it. Are you okay?"

"I'll be fine. I think I'll go work out. Take care, Spike."

"You too, Lyle. Thanks."

Fifteen minutes later, Puck comes out, "Bobby, you're next." He meets Spikes eyes. "Are you okay, Spike?"

"Yes. I'm fine," and she smiles.

"It looks to me like they want all the facts so they can bury the correct information."

She chuckles, "I don't want to know right now."

"I just want to prepare you for a 'no resolution' resolution."

"Eric, I fully understand the political ramifications of this situation."

"I know. I'm just not sure if you get the personal ramifications. The only justice you'll get happened out there."

"Eric, I'm mourning the loss of everyone."

"I am too, but you lost something as well. Are you sure you're okay?"

"Of course, I lost something. What are you trying to say?"

"Even though he wasn't fully successful, he violated you. And everyone knows he did."

"I know it's hard to understand, but I can handle what he tried to do to me. It's losing Mosey that's hard."

The door opens and Bobby walks out, "You're up, Skipper."

"Thank you, Bobby. I'm fine, Eric, really."

ADMIRAL'S CONFERENCE ROOM, USS CARL VINSON

1806, 15 January, 1942

Admiral Halsey, with two of his staff captains, sits at one side of a table with Captain Johnson and Captain Holtz. In chairs against the wall are the Admiral's legal officer, Lt. Bishop, the ships legal officer, Lt. Watson, and Naval Investigative Service (NIS) Special Agent Donald Matthew.

LCDR Hunt sits across the table and is winding down her statement about yesterday's events. "Sir, he was so focused on shooting us down, he forgot to look for the enemy. I told him he had an enemy on his six, but he couldn't hear me. The Japanese missile hit on his left engine, inducing a flat spin. They ejected at about 5,000 feet. We shot down the enemy fighter who shot him and noted his location for helicopter pickup."

Halsey says, "Thank you, Commander. Are there any questions, gentlemen?"

Captain Van Zandt asks, "When did you know Lt. Carleton was in the air?"

"I figured it out after a couple of calls for Felix 541 to return to base, sir."

"When did you know he was trying to kill you?"

"When I realized the plane on my six was a F-14, sir."

Johnson asks, "Why didn't you shoot him down? You had the shot and your finger was on the trigger, which is why we have gun camera footage."

"I couldn't, sir. It would have been murder."

Captain Miles says, "More like justifiable homicide, if you ask me."

"Is that a question, sir?"

Miles shakes his head, "No, a statement. I believe you acted admirably. More admirably than I would have under the circumstances."

"Sir, Lt. JG Boxter was also in that plane. He turned on his radar to warn us. He didn't deserve to die regardless of his pilot's actions."

Halsey says, "Captain Holtz? They're your people."

Holtz says, "Lt. Carleton's discipline problems and poor conduct in regards to women in uniform have already been discussed. The command believed that by removing him from Commander Hunt's chain of command, and, in essence, ordering him to have no contact with her, the problem could be managed. I did not anticipate that he was capable of such horrible conduct. The gun sight camera footage and statements from the other pilots and RIOs, and crew, corroborate Commander Hunt's testimony completely. The man is dead. What should we do now?"

Halsey asks, "Special Agent Matthew?"

Matthew says, "The knife that killed Chief White was handled by only one person, Lt. Carleton. The physical evidence at the scene: Chief White's wounds and the condition of Commander Hunt's flight suit all corroborate previous testimony. Furthermore, there is no contraindicative evidence. It is clear to me that Lt. Carleton, while in the act of committing aggravated rape, was interrupted by ADC Paul White, whom he attacked and killed. Carleton planned the attack and chose the location carefully, indicated by the note and the staged tool box. Had Chief White not interrupted him, it is clear to me that Lt. Carleton would have raped LCDR Hunt. The evidence and statements are sufficient to show that he attempted to kill LCDR Hunt in the air by cannon fire, and consequently, her RIO, Lt. JG Hawke."

Captain Johnson says, "The man was obsessed with Commander Hunt. His behavior degraded until he decided to kill her. His behavior is not due to the outside influence of any other person. His intent is now clear. His mental state is open to speculation but seems irrelevant at this time."

Halsey says, "I agree. I see only one more matter as to Lt. Carleton. Lieutenant Bishop, I believe the correct course is to submit the testimony and conclusions of this hearing into John Carleton's permanent record and close it as deceased before he could be brought to justice. I want the charges to be one count of attempted aggravated rape, one count of murder, and three counts of attempted murder."

Lt. Watson asks, "Three counts, sir?"

Halsey counts on his fingers, "Lieutenant Commander Hunt, her radar intercept officer, Lieutenant JG Hawke, and his own radar intercept officer, Lt. JG Boxter.

"Now, we need to discuss how we will deal with female servicemen going forward. I have a number of concerns that this type of thing may happen again." He pauses, "We have time to discuss that issue later. Now, to the matter of Commander Hunt. It is possible for me to close this record, but I fear too many people already know. What are your wishes, Commander?"

Sam says, "I'm not sure I understand what you mean, sir."

"Do you want us to lock up this event, keeping it secret in an attempt to protect your dignity?"

Sam shakes her head, "No, I think Lt. Carleton's behavior was an aberration. If women are going to serve in the United States Navy and be considered equals, they must accept that equal treatment means equal responsibility. I believe transparency is more important than my dignity, sir."

Halsey nods, "So see, his behavior as an aberration. I do have my doubts there. It seems to me that war brings out both the best and worst in people. You're not concerned that the event will color your leadership, and worse, the opinions of your subordinates?"

"No, sir."

"You are brand new in command, I'm not surprised at your confidence." He looks to the other panel members, "As the accused is deceased, I believe we should consider this matter closed." Then to Van Zandt, "Send it up to Nimitz."

He pauses, thinking, then continues, "The final issue is command policy as it pertains to the treatment of female sailors. I wish widest dissemination. Any deliberate mistreatment of female sailors under my command will be dealt with in the harshest way commensurate with the offense. Any commander failing to report mistreatment, or failing to follow this order, will be summarily stripped of all rank and privileges and dismissed. Questions, gentlemen?"

Sam raises her hand, "One, sir?"

"Yes, Commander?"

"Is it possible that Chief Paul White be buried with full honors as lost in battle? I'm asking for myself, but also for my squadron. He's a huge loss. He was a mentor and friend to us all."

"Absolutely. Chris, so note. Anything else?" When there is no response. "Then this matter is closed. Thank you all."

HUNT FARM, STONE MOUNTAIN, TENNESSEE

1115 local time, 16 January, 1942

At thirty-seven years old, Margaret Hunt is still very pretty. Her blonde hair is pulled back in a bun, and this chill morning she is wearing a grey wool skirt, cream blouse, and a navy-blue cardigan. Looking down at the picture sitting on the letter from the Department of the Navy, she's not sure she believes what she is seeing. Picking the picture up of the woman in an officer's uniform, she takes it to a daguerreotype on the wall. The resemblance between the woman in the picture in her hand and the woman in the daguerreotype is uncanny.

The woman on the wall is Melanie Hunt, her husband's grandmother. Melanie is a legend in the family, for it is said that she held off a company of union cavalry who were trying to take her last breeding stock of horses. She was alone with a shotgun, a dog, and two grooms. She didn't back down. She kept her horses.

And now, the Department of the Navy of the United States of America is trying to tell her that her granddaughter has come back in time on a naval vessel. It's so hard to believe. She picks up the letter and reads it again. "Well, she does look like a Hunt. If she has the same spirit as her great grandmother, she will win the war by herself." Sitting down at the table, she reads the letter again, and begins to write.

YOKOSUKA NAVAL BASE, TOKYO BAY, JAPAN

0845, 17 January, 1942

A grey Mercedes weaves between the still burning buildings and pulls to a stop. A captain steps forward and opens the door, and General Tojo steps out. He looks around, surveying the devastation, then, "Report, Captain."

Captain Himura says, "We have been hard hit, but we will recover. Four dry docks are damaged, three with ships in them. Dry dock two was badly hit, it will be many months before Atago can be freed from the debris and repaired. The battleship Yamashiro has been sunk in the bay. The carrier Hiryu was damaged at the pier. It sank but can be recovered and repaired. Our fuel supplies have been destroyed and the fuel stations have to be rebuilt. Much of our workshops and repair facilities are also damaged. We have 1,837 dead and many hundreds still missing, all trained and experienced workers."

Then they hear a distant boom and the roar of jets high overhead.

TOKYO BAY, 20,000 FEET AT MACH 2

Swede's F-14 carries a Tactical Airborne Reconnaissance Pod System (TARPS) and two sidewinders. Hot Pant's F-14 carries two AIM-7 Sparrow missiles and two AIM-9 Sidewinders. They fly loose deuce over Tokyo Bay. On intercom, Swede says, "Damn, Gandhi, we hit them hard."

"I know, but I see a missile system on a truck being moved. They are already repairing."

GQ, over the radio, "Swede, I see a group of officers in the navy yard, request permission to engage."

"Not the mission, GQ. We may need that ordinance to make it back home."

TOKYO BAY, YOSUKA NAVY YARD

General Tojo looks up, trying to make out the distant aircraft. When he spots the planes, he sees the distinctive triangle shape of an F-14 at high speed. "Captain, they return. Contact Chitose."

Captain Himura runs into a building as Major Ueno, Tojo's chief of staff says, "General, you must seek cover."

"No, I must watch and learn; only a mole hides in a hole."

IN THE AIR

Puffs of ack-ack bloom behind the planes as they make a gradual turn. Swede says, "Illuminate," and both aircraft turn on their radar. As they continue the turn, Gandhi says, "Swede, we have fast movers at 100 miles out, at 010."

GQ says, "We have company, two fast movers at 100 miles and angels 30."

"We see them, GQ. Time to go home." They continue the turn, then depart south east at high Mach.

Gandhi says, "Knight 1, Knight 309, feet wet and bringing company."

They continue at high Mach, burning fuel and slowly climbing, the Japanese F-15s in pursuit. 250 miles out to sea, they hear Puck, 100 miles ahead, "Illuminate."

Puck and Speedy turn on their radar, quickly acquiring the pursuing aircraft. They're on station at 400 knots and 40,000 feet, now 80 miles ahead of Swede's flight.

Puck says, "Spike, I have lock. They are 160 miles out at high Mach. We'll volley when in range."

"Okay, Puck."

Puck, on radio, "Speedy, we'll volley two each on my mark. You have right and I have left."

On intercom, "Spike, they're still boring in. Okay, good tone. Wait. Wait. Volley Fox 3." Spike and Thud pickle off four Phoenix missiles.

Swede and Hot Pants are still out of range of the Japanese AIM-7 missiles, as the AIM-54s bear down on the pursuing jets. The Phoenix's find their target as Swede and Hot Pants flash by and start to slow. One F-15 explodes and the other turns back.

Speedy says, "That's your kill, Puck. We were aiming at the other one."

Puck answers, "You got him, Speedy. There are parts falling off him." They watch as the crippled F-15 falls into the sea.

Spike and Thud are the air-fuel buddy stores, as well as air cover this day. Turning to catch up with the Swede and Hot Pants as they slow, they refuel the two thirsty Tomcats.

Two hundred miles east, the four Tomcats form up behind four Black Knights with more buddy stores and refuel. Then, the eight Tomcats continue south east, flying at most economical. Three hundred miles further and eight S-3 Screw Birds tank them up, again. Three hundred more miles and they are home, landing aboard the Carl Vinson. Sixteen aircraft are needed to push two over 1,000 miles for a supersonic reconnaissance pass.

CHAPTER 7

USS CARL VINSON, ELEVATOR 3

1400, 18 January, 1942

The crew stands at attention in working uniform. The officers are in dress uniform: Halsey, Johnson, Patterson, Tucker, Zacharias, Wakefield, Bentley, Holtz, Sherman, and Hunt. Chaplain Chandler says a brief prayer, and they read the names and home towns of the fallen as the boatswains lift each flag-draped board to tip a body over the side.

FC3 Bonnie Anderson, Long Beach, Washington, Carl Vinson

MM3 Robert Baker, Johnstown, Georgia, Dunlap

Lieutenant John Carleton, Allentown, Pennsylvania, Tomcatters

Ensign Ulster Carmello, Lyman, South Dakota, Fanning

GM3 Lindell Cartwright, Knoxville, Tennessee, Salt Lake City

Lieutenant JG, Brian Duncan, Bradenton, Florida, Salt Lake City

FC2 Christopher Ebbert, Albuquerque, New Mexico, Carl Vinson

GM1 Lincoln Edwards, Prestonburg, Kentucky, Salt Lake City

IC2 Michael Gilbertson, Balston Spa, New York, Salt Lake City

BT1 Albert Grady, Lineville, Alabama, Salt Lake City

Lieutenant Commander Peter Gregory, Fayetteville, North Carolina, Fife

BMSN Dwight Hughes, Rutland, Vermont, Salt Lake City

Lieutenant Commander Margaret Lafferty, Reading Pennsylvania, Fife

Commander James Lamoure, Chico, California, Fife

GMSN Nelson Lennon, Barnes, Wisconsin, Salt Lake City

BM2 Pepper Lewis, Houma, Louisiana, Fife

Lieutenant JG Larry Neel, Decatur, Illinois, Dunlap

Lieutenant John Patterson, Savanna, Georgia, Fanning

Lieutenant Walter Jones, Downey, California, Fife

Ensign Hank Teal, Enterprise, Alabama, Salt Lake City

ADC Paul White, Flagstaff, Arizona, Black Knights

After the names are read, Chaplain Perry prays: "Lord, we surrender the bodies of these brave sailors to the deep, knowing that they rest with you. We ask that you lift up those lost over enemy territory. Please keep them safe and hold them close. In the name of the Our Lord, Jesus Christ, we all say, Amen."

After a moment, they all head back into the ship and Captain Johnson walks up to Sam, "Commander?"

She salutes, "Yes, sir."

"I've been thinking. The day we came back in time, you manned the bridge for me. Are you interested in getting your SWO?"

"Sir?"

"Surface Warfare Officer. You know, someday you are going to command one of these. It would be handy to know how to drive one."

"Sir? Really? Me?"

"You're a good officer, a gifted pilot, and you have a level head. Yes, you. Do you want to earn your SWO?"

"Yes, sir. I would be honored."

"Good. You'll be on the watch bill starting tomorrow. I will send over the books." Smiling, he turns and walks away.

Sam, stunned, watches him leave, "My God, what have I gotten into?"

WARDROOM 1, USS CARL VINSON

1530, 1800 January, 1942

The captains and XOs from all the commands in the battle group quietly find their seats. Sam walks to the rear and sits next to LCDR Jeremy 'Frosty' Winters, CO of the Fighting Red Cocks. He looks her in the eye, "How are you, Commander?"

"I'm fine, Frosty. Really, I am."

Frosty starts to speak and LCDR Todd 'Groovy' Miller, CO of the Tomcatters joins them, "Is this seat taken?"

Sam smiles, "No, please. How are you?"

"Good, I'm getting worried about resupply, though."

Frosty says, "Yeah, but we are heading home. Hopefully it will sort itself out before we fight again."

Sam asks, "Where did you hear we are going home?"

Frosty looks at her, "Did you get a good look at the Long Beach? The Fife? We got hammered in the missile attack. We have to go home and make repairs."

She says, "Yes, they do, but we don't. We lost a CIWS, but other than that, we're still ready to fight."

Groovy says, "We need to get a source for parts though. Especially our electronics."

Sam replies, "Have my guys shared the card testing rig they came up with?"

Before Groovy can answer, Admiral Halsey and his staff walk in, "Attention on deck!" They all stand.

Halsey walks to the front of the wardroom, "Fellas, we've done well, really well. We made the Japs bleed. Old Tojo is probably crying himself to sleep at night. But, let's not kid ourselves, we still have a lot of fighting in front of us.

"Here is where we stand," he points at a map. "We are here, about 1300 nautical miles from Japan. Tomorrow we will be splitting the battlegroup. The Enterprise, San Francisco, Long Beach, Mugford, Anderson, and Kaiser will continue east and meet up with the Saratoga Task Force here. The Carl Vinson will turn south. We will swing by Wake and see how our boys are doing, then hit the Marshalls on our way to Australia. In Australia, we will make repairs and standby for further orders. Questions?"

Commander Wakefield stands, "Sir, does the Camden have enough JP-5 to get us there?"

"Good question. The Kaiser will transfer all its remaining JP-5 stores to the Camden before we split."

Captain Tenzar asks, "Sir, Vinson is down a CIWS. If we can figure out a way to remove it at sea, it can have one of mine seeing as I'll be going into the yards anyway."

"Good idea. How could it be done? Can a helicopter lift the thing off the boat?"

Commander Crocker says, "Yes, sir, as long as the CIWS is broken down into bite size pieces."

Halsey looks at Captain Johnson. Johnson says, "It's a good idea."

ADMIRAL'S CONFERENCE ROOM

1655, 18 January, 1942

LCDR Brewster Flanagan, the Salt Lake City's CHENG, steps into Admiral Halsey's conference room, "You wished to see me, sir?"

Halsey, sitting with his chief of staff, Captain Miles, says, "Yes, Commander. Grab a cup of coffee and have a seat."

When Flanagan is settled, Halsey says, "I've read Captain Zacharias' report on the loss of your ship. You have nothing to be ashamed of or to regret. That isn't why I want to see you."

"Yes, sir."

"My question is simple; can you serve under a female commander?"

"Um, sir, I guess so. As long as she, um, she's competent. I don't see that it would matter much. It would take some getting used to, though."

"Of course, it would. It means giving up your survivor leave as well, and I know that is a sacrifice. Are you willing to tackle learning a whole new type of propulsion plant from her, while running the same plant?"

"Sir, does she know what she is talking about?"

"I'm told she's a systems expert. The Fife was decapitated by a missile. The present commander was a division officer for their number two propulsion plant and the senior officer who survived. She saved her ship, and I gave her command. She needs a chief engineer. I want you.

"You did well on the Salt Lake City. Elias says great things about you. I can't have you being a problem, though. Understand, you will have females under your leadership, as well. Will you do it?"

"Yes, sir. Can I meet her?"

"I've already discussed this with her. Captain Miles, would you invite Commander Wakefield in?" Miles leaves and returns a few moments later with Commander Wakefield, still in her dress blues. Halsey stands, "Commander Wakefield, this is LCDR Flanagan, your new engineer."

Wakefield gives Flanagan a measuring look, "Welcome aboard the USS Fife, Commander. You'll have your work cut out for you."

"Admiral Halsey says it's a new type of plant."

"Yes, gas turbine. Instead of steam, we use jet engines similar to those used by the aircraft the Vinson flies. It's a whole new set of procedures and equipment you need to learn."

"Do you have problems with men and women, um, you know?"

"Of course, it happens now and again. When it does happen, we punish the perpetrators so severely it deters it for a time. But, our first priority is to put together a temporary bridge. We are building what amounts to a tent right now, but it is what we have." She turns to Admiral Halsey, "Sir, I have no doubt that LCDR is a phenomenal chief engineer. But I think he could serve me better as the XO. It would also benefit his career rather than repeating an assignment."

Halsey smiles, "I do see your point. Approved. Now if you two could excuse me."

Once they are out the door, Flanagan says, "Thank you, Captain."

She smiles, still not used to being called that, "I've heard what you did for the Salt Lake City. You're both thoughtful and tenacious. We will need that. You also have more practical leadership experience than I do. We'll get to know each other better soon enough. Now we have new crew mustering in hangar bay two. If you can attend to that, I need to talk to Captain Johnson. He commands the carrier we are on."

"Yes, ma'am."

Wakefield puts out her hand, "Thank you. I look forward to working with you, Commander."

HANGAR BAY 3, USS CARL VINSON

1703, 18 January, 1942

Spike, walks through the hangar bay, weaving around her squadron aircraft. The bay is crowded with F-14s needing repair and maintenance. Three of her aircraft have engines removed, two have radomes open, and another has its gun system out. With the Enterprise once again handling most of the patrolling, they have birds on ready five, but none flying. AN3 Greg 'Duck' Newburg approaches, looking down with his hands in his pockets, then looks up. "Ma'am, I know you're busy, but, um."

"Yes, what can I do for you, Duck?"

"Well, ma'am, it's Ham, um, MM1 Hammond. With all the new people hurt, they kind of kicked him out of medical, again. And now, he don't got a division. They've given him orders for the Fife, ma'am. He's all burned up, ma'am. They can't drag him over there. Can he work with us?" He looks at her, eyes full of hope.

She nods, "Yeah, sure. I'll call up Halsey's staff. It's probably a mix up. How's he doing, by the way? I know he saved our berthing."

"Oh, thank you, ma'am. Thank you. He's the hardest worker ever. He still can't do much…but, thank you."

She smiles, "Greg, it's not a problem. I'll take care of it. Send him to see Senior Chief Bond. He'll find a place for your friend."

HANGAR BAY 2

1712, 18 January, 1942

BT3 Donny Petrakis, from the Stoddert, stands with a group of sailors, some from 1942, who served on vessels just recently lost. He's in his working uniform with his sea bag next to him. He doesn't have much, but it's something. A young sailor with bushy black hair and a stained hat approaches reading his uniform, "Hey, Petty Officer Petrakis, where you from?"

Donny reads the sailors uniform, "Miami, Florida. How about you, um, Petrakis?"

Seamen John Petrakis says, "Oh, I thought we might be related. I'm from Philly."

Donny grins, "My grandma lives in Philly, on 18th Street."

"What's her name?"

"Linda. This is getting weird."

"Yep, my brother Ted married Linda. I'm your great uncle John."

"How old are you?"

"Eighteen."

"This is nuts, my great uncle John, um, shit. You died in the battle of San Bernardino Strait."

"I didn't need to know that."

"Sorry, you transferring to Fife?"

"Yeah, you too?"

Donny says, "Yep. You know, everything is changed. There might not even be a battle of San Bernardino Strait, so I guess you're okay."

CHAPTER 8

BRIDGE, USS CARL VINSON

0720, 21 January, 1942

Sam, wearing khaki, is standing watch with binoculars hanging from her neck. Her job is making sure the other ships are on station. Working on her SWO, she is the conning officer under instruction watch. Fluffy enters the bridge in his flight deck uniform and the OOD, Lt. Sawyer says, "No flight deck uniforms on the bridge, Senior Chief."

Fluffy says, "Yes, ma'am," and gives Sam an inquiring look.

She mouths the word, "Later."

He shakes his head and leaves.

Sawyer asks, "One of yours, Commander?"

"Yes, my senior enlisted advisor."

"You get relieved in 10 minutes."

"Yes, I know. It'll wait."

Commander Todd "Groovy" Miller, of the Tomcatters, walks in in his khakis, "Request to enter the bridge to relieve the watch."

Sawyer says, "Enter."

A few minutes later Sam is walking down the flights of stairs from the bridge. She finds Fluffy in the ready room, "What is it, Fluffy?"

"Ma'am, what are you doing standing bridge watches? Fuck the black shoe Navy."

She smiles, "Fluffy, how many supercarriers does the navy have right now?"

"Us. Just us, ma'am."

"True. How many do you suppose the navy will have by the end of the war?"

"I don't know, ma'am. It takes years to build one, so maybe two."

"One of the reasons it takes so long is congress stretches out funding. They are incredibly complex, especially the nuclear carriers. My guess, ten or more. We are at war and these ships are critical."

"That will be something, ma'am."

"Yes, it will be. Who do you suppose will command them?"

"Oh shit, ma'am. I'm sorry. You're preparing for command."

"Johnson thinks it's a good idea. The other squadron commanders are working on their SWO's, too."

Swede walks over, "Does Halsey know?"

"I didn't ask."

Fluffy, "Oh, by the way, ma'am. We've settled on a winner."

"Winner? What?"

"The squadron logo contest," and Fluffy grins. "We've chosen what we think is the best" He hands over two papers. One is the current logo with the sword and shield of the knight grounded. The new logo is identical, except the shield on the left arm is raised, and the sword in the right hand is poised to attack. "I figure this keeps with the tradition but reflects that we're at war."

"I take it the others were a little more flamboyant. Who came up with this?"

"They're from your old division, Lori Givens and Greg Newburg. He designed it and she did the drawing."

Sam nods, "I like it. Well, when do we present it to the squadron?"

"I have the sail loft working on a flag. It should be ready in a day or two. We'll do it then."

"Thank you, Senior. I appreciate this. I'll have dinner with the two that night. By the way, which plane should it go on?"

"Everyone's, ma'am. But I think Thud should fly the show bird. He has the most kills besides you."

"Good idea, I like it."

"No, problem. By the way, the chief's mess is throwing an ice cream social tonight on the aft mess decks. You ought to come down. You're looking a little thin."

Spike grins, "Get out of here."

USS CARL VINSON, PORT BEAM

1100, 21 January, 1942

A rigid hull inflatable boat, RHIB, pounds through the seas toward two surfaced submarines, the USS Dolphin and the USS Sturgeon. The RHIB is piled with five-gallon tubs of ice cream. It gets to the Dolphin first where two men in flight suits are on deck with the crew. ENS Hugo

'Don' Alphonza, pilot of Viceroy 7, shakes Lt. Rainer's and Lt. JG Porter's hands, "Thank you so much for saving us from certain death."

Rainer smiles, "I'm glad we were able to wiggle our way into Tokyo Bay to get you."

ENS Butch 'Screws' Phillips, Viceroy 7's bombardier, shakes their hands, "You guys kick butt."

Porter says, "It was clever to click your belt buckle against your gun in 'a shave and a haircut'. It's how we heard you."

They each salute Lt. Rainer and the ship and are helped into the RHIB while the RHIB's crew hand up tubs of ice cream. It's a tradition as old as naval aviation. The RHIB then maneuvers to the Sturgeon as the two airmen wave to their rescuers.

On the deck of the Sturgeon are some of its crew and its captain and XO, LCDR A.D. Barnes and Lt. JG Jarvis. Standing with them are ENS Patrick 'Bug' Ulster, pilot of Knight 101, his RIO Lt. JG Hyam 'Joker' Alberts, Lt. Laramie 'Six Gun' Morrison, of Beefeater 9, and ENS Jebediah 'Skeeter' McAllister, of the Red Cocks.

They shake the submariner's hands, "Thank you, Commander, Lieutenant. We thought we were fish food for sure," says Ulster.

Barnes replies, "Our pleasure, but don't make it a habit, okay?"

Alberts says, "You guys are ballsy to fight a war in one of these."

Jarvis says, "Coming from someone who flies a craft with no visible means of support, I'll take that as a compliment."

Morrison says, "I owe my life to you fella's. It's not a debt I will forget."

Barnes replies, "We were just glad we found you. Try to duck next time."

McAllister, still shaking Barnes hand, "I appreciate what you and your fine crew have done. You make Mamma Skeeter very happy."

The four men climb aboard the RHIB and help hand up the ice cream to their rescuers. The RHIB pounds back to the port side of the Vinson where it accepts a bowline and a large hook, which are hooked to a cleat and a lifting eye. Then, as the boat is lifted out of the water, the coxswain secures the motor and they all grab hold of monkey lines in case the boat falls. It is lifted 60 feet to its mount on the mid-port sponson.

When they get out of the RHIB, they walk into a wall of cheering Vinson sailors. Halsey, Johnson, and all of the squadron commanders are at the head of the line. Ensign Ulster sees Spike, "I'm sorry I lost the bird, ma'am."

Spike pulls him and Joker into a hug, "I'm just glad you're back. Welcome home."

BLACK KNIGHTS CO'S OFFICE

1730, 21 January, 1942

Spike is buried in award package paperwork, typing a draft for the tenth time, when her door opens. Gloria walks in and sets a bowl of ice cream in front of her, "Rocky road, right?"

Sam looks up, startled, "Yeah, wow, thanks." The ice cream has extra fudge, almond sprinkles, whipped cream, and a cherry on top.

Gloria sits down, removing papers from a chair, "Just sucking up to the boss. By the way, Bug and Joker have been cleared by medical." Gloria takes a bite of her ice cream, luxuriating in the taste.

"That's good to hear. I was worried about them. I know we all were." They eat in silence. Sam asks, "What are you having?"

"Chocolate overload: chocolate ice cream with chocolate chunks and hot fudge, pure heaven."

Sam laughs, "Thank you."

"You know, you're holing up in your office again. What's the deal?"

"The deadline for all the awards is tomorrow morning."

"Why so soon?"

"Don't know. I presume Papa has his reasons."

"Why are you doing it alone? It's like crunch time in college. Let me call the guys up and we can pound it out and get a decent night's sleep. You could use one."

"The guys are among the awardees."

"Of course, they are. Just don't give them their own. You know, you aren't the Lone Ranger."

Sam cocks her head and grins, "Okay." She picks up a stack of files, "Fine, here."

BLACK KNIGHT READY ROOM

2030, 21 January, 1942

Hot Pants, Swede, Thud, Puck, Gandhi, GQ, and Speedy are at desks pounding away on typewriters. Moody Blues is blaring from a boom box in the corner and empty ice cream bowls are everywhere. Swede asks, "How do you spell 'exemplary'?"

Absently, without looking up, Spike spells it for him.

Then Thud asks, "Can I use the word 'studly'?"

Everyone looks up. Hot Pants says, "Say the word in context, Thud."

"In a studly maneuver, he succeeded in shooting down two aircraft in a single pass."

Spike asks, "Whose file do you have?"

Thud turns red, "Um, Swede's."

Spike smiles, "Skilled maneuver, Frank."

Swede says, "You mean, I'm not studly, boss?"

Spike shakes her head, smiling, "I'm not touching that." She goes back to work.

WARDROOM 1, USS CARL VINSON

1600, 24 January, 1942

LCDR Hunt walks into wardroom 1, in her undress blues. Following her in are Airmen Lori Givens and Greg Newburg, also in their dress uniforms. Greg had to borrow his, but it has his green airman stripes and his purple heart. They look around tentatively, a bit overwhelmed. A mess attendant approaches and bows slightly, "Commander, guests, please, a table is this way."

Sam says, "Thank you." They are led to a six-person table near the front.

"What would you wish to drink?"

Sam says, "Coffee, please. You two?"

Lori squeaks, "Milk, please."

Greg asks, "Do you have root beer?"

The mess attendant says, "Yes, we do. One moment," leaving a one-page menu with them.

Lori looks at Sam, "You get real waiters here?"

"Yes, Lori, but do you notice, there are no flight suits down here?" Lori and Greg look around and nod. "They're not allowed. That's why I normally eat in wardroom 3, which is about the same as your mess decks." The mess attendant returns with their drinks, and Spike says, "The meat loaf, potatoes, and greens, with a salad, ranch, please."

"Greg nods, "Um, me too.""

Lori says, "Uh huh, yeah, me too."

Greg looks at Lori, "This is cool, scary, but cool."

Lori just smiles.

The air boss, Commander Forrester approaches, "May I join you and your guests, Commander?"

The three stand, and Spike says, "Certainly. Commander Forrester, may I introduce Airman Lori Givens and Airman Greg Newburg. They won the contest for a new tail design for the Black Knights."

He shakes both their hands, "I heard, and I like it." He sits down.

Lori whispers to Greg, "Oh my God, we are so dead."

Forrester says, "I only chew up airman on the flight deck. Away from PRIFLY I'm somewhat civilized. I've been accused of being nice...once."

Sam chuckles and Lori turns red. The attendant approaches and Forrester orders. He asks, "How did you come up with your design, just having the knight pick up his shield and sword?"

Greg smiles at Lori, "I figured that we were fighting a war, sir. You don't fight a war with your weapons sitting on the ground. Lori drew it up, really cool."

"Greg, how did you come by the purple heart."

Greg looks at him and lowers his head. Spike says, "He's a survivor of the Stoddert, sir. Bad burns from engine room 2. He wouldn't leave his injured comrades. He stayed with them on the fan tail, waving for a chopper. When we picked them up, he wouldn't board the bird until the rest of his friends were picked up. I'm proud to have him in my squadron."

"Oh, is he the one who annoyed medical? I heard about that. What happened to the rest of the guys?"

Greg answers, "All of them died that night, except for Ham, sir. Ham pulled through and he's a Black Knight now like me. He put the fires out in the forward sponson after we was hit by the missile. Ham is a hero, sir, a real hero."

"Oh, wow," Forrester to Sam, "Who's Ham?"

"Machinist Mate First Class Oscar Hammond, sir. Greg's right. Ham was born with an overabundance of the hero gene. He was in our squadron berthing during the attack because he can't effectively use his hands. They were badly burned pulling all the watch standers out of the engine room on Stoddert. When the Vinson was hit, he manned a hose, by himself, and put out the fires. He saved our berthing and saved the ship a lot of damage."

"Wow. You know the O-2 plant was right below where the missile hit. If the fire had reached it, the whole ship could have been lost. I hope you wrote him up."

"Oh, yes. Twice."

The mess attendant delivers their meals on porcelain plates. One of the rules in the Navy is that the officers must eat the same food served to the enlisted crew. It isn't prepared quite the same way, though. Lori and Greg look surprised at the food. Lori asks, "Ma'am, may we say grace, please?"

"Certainly, Lori. Would you like to lead?"

"Um, okay, sure. We hold hands at our house." She reaches for Greg's hand, then, tentatively, for Forrester's. He takes her hand smiling and takes Sam's. She takes Greg's, and they bow their heads. "Lord, thank you for this day. Thank you for this food. Thank you for bringing us to victory. In your Holy name, Amen."

Forrester says, "That was nice, Lori. Thank you."

Lori blushes, "Thank you, sir."

WASHINGTON NAVAL YARD, PLANNING OFFICE

1000 local time, 23 January, 1942

Captain Warren stands as the Admirals walk into the conference room: Admiral King (CNO), Admiral Peterson (NAVSEA COMMAND), Admiral Klindt (NAVSEA 08), Admiral Nimitz (CINCPAC), Admiral Lewis (CINCLANT). "Sirs, thank you for coming. I'll get right to it. In light of the new technology we have brought to the table, I have a number of recommended ship building changes."

Admiral Peterson asks, "So, you want to cancel all the battleships in favor of carriers, right?"

Warren looks at him surprised, "No, sir. The Iowa, New Jersey, Missouri, and Wisconsin have progressed to the point that they should be completed as battleships. The other two hulls just laid should be converted to carriers, though. I am also recommending we build purpose-built supercarriers, three at a time. If we focus on Kaiser type modular design, we can build the ships more quickly. Still, if we are to complete them in time to impact the war, we must start immediately and put financial and manpower focus on the project. This could impact the big gun projects."

Admiral King asks, "Okay, what about the battleships? Do they have a role?"

"Yes, sir. The battleships are used for shore bombardment, AAW screen, and anti-surface. I recommend more gun tubes, not less. We should complete the four Iowa class with integrated missile armament. We should also make an eight-ship class of battle cruisers."

King asks, "Why battle cruisers? If you want guns, the battle cruiser uses an as yet untested 12-inch gun."

"Yes, sir, but it could be mounted with double 16-inch turrets instead. It would be six guns, rather than nine, but they would use common ammunition trains and spare parts."

Admiral Preston asks, "What about the Essex class?"

Warren replies, "We reconfigure as amphibious and anti-submarine carriers using helicopters. We will want a new class with a well deck."

Nimitz asks, "A well deck? What are you talking about?"

Warren says, "A ship with ballast tanks that can be filled to put the rear in the water to float amphibious craft out. It's way safer than climbing down cargo nets."

King says, "All Lee talks about are carrier decks. How long until we can give him what he needs?"

"The carrier based on the battleship hull should be completed in about 10 to 12 months. The new carriers are about a year and a half out. We'll be building on both coasts and making at least three at once. The slipway at Bremerton is already being configured."

Peterson says, "Those ships are outside of 90,000 tons. You propose to launch them on slipway? That's madness."

"Sir, we must have the ships. No dry dock exists that can accommodate them. Building dry docks that could, would set back the program six months to a year. We will be building those dry docks, but we have to get these ships built as soon as possible. So, we must build on slipways."

King asks, "Is that how the Vinson was built?"

"No, sir, but right now, there is no other way."

"Have you run the numbers? Can it be done?"

"Yes, sir. There are dangers. The staff at Puget Sound have helped me a lot."

Peterson says, "I'm all ears."

"We will put a number of tugs tied together with a line reeved through pullies to the bow. As the ship picks up speed, they will power up to slow her down."

Heads nod, and King says, "What about the submarines, destroyers, and cruisers?"

"We remove mount 3 and 4 from the Fletcher class and install a Mark-13 missile launcher and a CIWS. We have good blueprints, and we can retrofit the launcher to existing vessels. For the cruisers, we add vertical launchers with search and guidance radar, along with

CIWS and torpedoes. As for subs, Admiral Klindt has that area. The new fleet subs will be revolutionary."

CHAPTER 9

ADMIRAL'S OFFICE, USS CARL VINSON

1634, 25 January, 1942

Captain Johnson and Captain Holtz walk into the admiral's office carrying several binders. Johnson says, "Admiral, we have the awards package ready for review."

Halsey says, "Set it down so I can have a look at it."

Halsey reads the cover sheet, then looks up, "Captain, what is a Navy Achievement Medal, and why are we giving out more than a hundred of them?"

Johnson is struck dumb, "Uh, shit, sir. I bet half the awards we are putting in for don't exist. Hell, half the awards I wear don't exist. I didn't think of that, sir. We have to do something for the men. Our guys pretty much expect it. The survivors of the Stoddert need to be recognized as well. Most of them are here, or on the Fife. There are two posthumous CMH packages that need to be sent up for Commander Douglas and Lt. Commander Hubler, CO and CHENG of the Stoddert."

Halsey leans back in his chair, "Grab some coffee, I think I need a history lesson."

Over an hour later, the three men are eating dinner and still pouring over the paperwork. Halsey finally says,

"Captain, I think we've got it. Let the other unit commanders know the plan. I will shoot this up for approval."

HUNT FARM, STONE MOUNTAIN TENNESSEE

1015, 28 January, 1942

Margaret Hunt reads the letter she's received from the office of Senator Tom Stewart.

Dear Mrs. Hunt,

At this time, Senator Tom Stewart can confirm that your granddaughter, Lieutenant Commander Samantha Leigh Hunt was among those sailors and airman, which through means unknown at this time, traveled back in time from 1990 to 1941.

She is a commissioned officer serving as commanding officer of VF-154. VF-154 is, as we understand, a combatant aircraft squadron. We were further informed that her role, besides that of officer in command, is as a pilot. The Navy informed our office that as of January 10, 1942, she has thirty-three confirmed aerial kills.

Her address is: VF154, NAV-AIR 02, Navy Department, Washington, DC. By writing to the address provided, your letters will be forwarded to whatever location she is serving.

Thank you for writing with your concerns.

Sincerely,

David Pruist

Assistant to Senator Tom Stewart

She's sitting in the kitchen, contemplating the letter, when her husband, Leigh Robert Hunt walks in. He pours himself a cup of coffee, saying, "I fixed the fence in the north pasture." He turns to look at his wife, "What is it, Darlin'?"

"I just got a letter from Senator Stewart's office. It seems we do, indeed, have a granddaughter serving in the Navy."

"Well, she hasn't written you back. Seems her family ain't all that important to her."

"We don't know that, Leigh. It said she's a pilot fighting the Japanese. It could take Lord knows how long for her to get my letter and send a reply."

"I suppose. So, she's a pilot? What kinda woman would put herself in such a position? Good Lord, a proper girl would be caring for the farm and kids while her man does the fighting."

"Your grandmother Melanie did her share of fighting in the Civil War, so you've said. Seems to me you're right proud of Grandma Melanie. Now, why shouldn't we be proud of this Hunt from the future. It says she's shot down thirty-three Japanese planes. Seems to me that is something to be proud of."

"Thirty-three planes? Good Lord, the Red Baron shot down eighty-nine over a whole war, and this war is just getting started. Maybe I should write her, too. We ought to be clear that she is welcome with her family."

KNIGHT 1, 36,000 FEET AND 200 MILES EAST OF WAKE ISLAND

0600, 29 January, 1942

The ocean below is that shimmery blue only possible in the South Pacific. As Spike's F-14 cuts through the skies, she can't suppress a smile, "Puck, it's awesome to be back in the air."

"Yeah, I miss this. Since you've been skipper, we hardly ever get to fly."

"It's not just that, we have to conserve fuel. But I know what you mean. You know, Puck, I'm starting to forget about home."

"You mean, 1990 home, or just America, period?"

"Puck, I remember America, it's just, Tennessee seems so far away. It's like the whole thing is a dream."

"Spike, picking up blips on radar. Mostly surface, okay, we have a strike force out there."

"Call it in, Puck." Spike wiggles the wings of her bird to get Thud's attention.

Puck on radio, "Gold Eagle, Knight 1. There is a surface force 380 miles west of Wake Island. I count 28 vessels, say again, two, eight vessels. Request permission to close and investigate."

"Knight 1, Gold Eagle. You are cleared to close and investigate. Engage any flat tops identified."

"Gold Eagle, Knight 1, acknowledged. Knight 212 roll in, loose deuce. Let's see what we have."

Speedy replies, "Roger, Puck. We're right with you." The two F-14's invert and dive, running their engines at most economical speed, the aircraft soon break the speed of sound, exchanging altitude for speed. Closing at 900 knots, the ships soon heave into view. What were mere smudges, soon become four aircraft carriers surrounded by escorting vessels and a swarm of zero fighters.

Spike, "Puck, let's see if we can get in and out before the zeros can be a problem."

"Spike, I want to make a pass to be sure they are Japanese."

"Okay, tell Speedy."

"Speedy, Puck, weapons tight until we make a positive ID."

"Puck, Speedy, roger, weapons tight."

COMBAT, USS CARL VINSON, 500 MILES SOUTH OF WAKE ISLAND

Halsey says, "Captain, why are they doing a dry pass? I told them to hit the carriers."

"Yes, sir. They're just making sure, being cautious."

"I don't want cautious. I want the carriers sunk. Launch one of your alpha strikes and tell them to hit the carriers. The Japanese will pay for Pearl Harbor today."

Johnson picks up a phone, "Launch an alpha. Anti-surface, about 700 miles north west. Tell Knight flight one, the carriers are hostile."

KNIGHT 1, OVER JAPANESE STRIKE GROUP

As they close, more and more details appear on the four ships, the big red ball clearly visible on the flight decks. Puck says, "Well, boss, they're Japs."

Spike pulls back on the stick, sending her fighter climbing to a higher altitude, as ack-ack starts exploding well behind them. "Okay, Puck. We call it in, then attack." A Zero crosses her path and she applies a little rudder, squeezing off rounds from her guns. The Zero catches fire, rolls and falls into the sea.

"Knight 1, Gold Eagle, engage the carriers. We have confirmation they are hostile."

As they pass 28,000 feet, Puck on radio, "Gold Eagle, Knight 1, we are engaging. We confirm, four Japanese flat tops. Two are the Akagi and the Kaga. I'm not sure about the others."

"Knight 1, Gold Eagle, hit the flat tops on the flight deck. Destroy the decks and as many aircraft as you can. We are launching support."

"Knight 1, Knight 212, I see another group of ships just to the east of Wake."

"Speedy, Puck, how many do you see?"

"About twenty."

"Knight 1, Gold Eagle. Focus on the carriers. We will address the others later."

"Acknowledge, Gold Eagle, flat tops first."

Spike says, "Fuck, Puck. Those other ships are probably amphibs."

"I know, Sam. We have our marching orders." Then on radio, "Speedy, rolling in."

The fighters dive directly on the ships, Puck says, "I have a good lock." Then on radio, "Fox 1. Fox 1."

Spike pulls the trigger on two AIM-7 Sparrow missiles. They streak toward two of the carriers as more ack-ack blossoms behind the supersonic fighters. Thud, on her right, pickles off three, then both aircraft are pulling out, skimming the waves, and starting the climb back for altitude. Two Zero's attempt to engage, but the F-14s are moving so fast, they can't turn in time. Behind them balls of flame ignite on three of the four carriers.

As they climb out, Spike rolls her bird to the left, flying toward Wake Island. She continues to climb, passing 20, 25, then 30,000 feet as she levels off. "Puck, check those boats out with the camera. What do we have?"

"You're right, Spike. They're amphibious, four with escorts. I count one, no two battleships or heavy cruisers."

Spike orients toward the amphibs, "We have to cover the Marines."

"Puck, Speedy. What are we doing?"

"Just stay on our wing, Speedy. If we hit the transports before they finish unloading, the Marines might be able to hold the island."

"Knight 1, Gold Eagle, mark the status of the aircraft carriers."

"Gold Eagle, Knight 1. Three out of four are on fire. The transports are unloading troops. We have to hit them now."

"Knight 1, Gold Eagle, acknowledge. Carry on."

COMBAT, USS CARL VINSON

Halsey picks up a phone, "Strike, why did you just approve a divert?"

Captain Holtz answers, "Sir, we are not there. I trust my pilot's judgement. If Spike says they need to hit the transports now, we should follow her lead."

"Bullshit. We destroy the carriers and they lose all air support. The marines will have to wait."

"Shall I call them back, sir?"

"No, but remind them what orders are when they return."

KNIGHT FLIGHT CLOSING THE INVASION FLEET, WAKE ISLAND

"Puck, do we have lock?"

"Just a sec." Then on radio, "Speedy, you take the two transports on the left. Fox 1. Fox 1."

Spike pickles off two AIM-7s. The supersonic missiles fly straight on to the transports as they sit nearly stopped and offloading soldiers onto the waiting boats. One hits the southernmost ship and the other hits the second, just to the north. Loaded with, men, supplies, weapons, ammunition, and fuel they burst into flames. As Spike pulls out, she fires a quick burst with her guns, hitting one of the landing boats heading for the atoll.

Dozens of boats are slowly making their way to the island beaches. As they climb out, black puffs of anti-aircraft fire appear from the escort ships below. Puck says, "Well, I would say, that pissed them off."

"Let's see how many of the boats we can take out before they hit shore."

"Speedy, Puck, we're rolling back in."

A handful of Zero's break off their attack on the island to engage the fighters but can't get to them.

"Puck, Speedy, we are sans AIM-7s. Switching to guns." As they line up for the next pass, they hear F-18s from the Vinson organizing the attack on the carriers.

They line up a pass on the bobbing wooden boats, difficult targets in the clear blue waters. Quick bursts of their guns and several boats are stopped, their engines burning. A Zero pulls toward them, and Thud destroys it. Again, they make a pass on the boats, and again, can only hit a few. As Spike fires on her seventh boat, she runs out of ammo.

"Shit, Puck. Our guns are dry. Maybe we can use our sonic boom to scare them."

"Spike, we're done. We need to get back to the ship."

"But Puck, I could use our exhaust. Maybe I can catch one of them on fire."

"Spike, we're bingo fuel. It's time to take it home. What's with you?"

"Alright. Tell Speedy it's time to go home."

As they climb out and head for home on the Carl Vinson, Puck asks, "Sam, what got into you? It was personal. Like they were killing your mom."

"Eric, my dad might be down there. They reinforced Wake, remember? I don't know where he is."

"Okay, Sam, I get it. We did what we could, now trust to the rest of the air wing. Trust those Marines to kick all the ass Marines always do."

CHAPTER 10

DACHA NEAR GZHEL USSR

The command track comes to a stop in the yard of the dacha just as the sun rises. It is a large home, no doubt built for some noble in Czarist times. Colonel General Kryukov steps out of the track and sees a scene of carnage in the yard. The guns of the Hind helicopters and the machine guns of his soldiers left bodies strewn everywhere. Captain Petrov, a Spetsnaz team leader approaches and salutes, "Comrade General it is done. If you come this way, I will show you."

Kryukov returns the salute and silently follows. He steps over the bodies and enters the residence. They walk through an entryway and up the grand staircase to a bedroom. Lying on the bed, gasping for breath, is Stalin. Their eyes meet. "Why?"

Kryukov says, "Your fear and incompetence cost us the Motherland. In defeating the Germans, you destroyed us. We fought the Americans, the West, but in the end, it was all lost. I will restore our Motherland to its proper place of greatness." He draws his side arm, points it at Stalin's head, and pulls the trigger. To the captain, "Thank you. Your service to me today is greatly appreciated. It was a distasteful task performed to perfection. Gather up your men. I will have need of them later."

SMITHSON FARM, GORST, WASHINGTON STATE

Shawn Hughes watches the dust trail of the old Ford driving away from his farm. Earlier this afternoon he'd signed the deed papers, signed the loan, and took custody of his farm. His farm. It would take some getting used to. As he watches the realtor drive away, he muses, "Well, you did it this time, Shawn. You bought the farm." He laughs.

Across the Sinclair Inlet he can see the shipyard. The low tide has exposed a few hundred yards of mud. The realtor had made it clear that this farm was useless to the navy. But, to him, it was very useful. Oh, yes. Very useful. Thirty acres of overgrown blackberry bushes with a road and a rail line right there. Enough.

He opens the rickety screen door and walks into the kitchen. They'd left a table and two chairs, so he pulls out a chair, lays his brief case on the table, and sits down. He pulls out paper and a pen and starts a letter.

Dear Samantha…

CAG'S OFFICE, USS CARL VINSON

1411, 29 January, 1942

Spike walks into Holtz's office, "Boss, why the hell were we going after some antiquated, pipsqueak, irrelevant aircraft carriers when there was an invasion fleet about to land thousands of fucking troops on Wake Island? I thought it was our job to protect the Marines."

Papa says, "Spike, calm down."

"Papa, it was bullshit. I don't get it."

From behind her she hears the distinctive voice of Admiral 'Bull' Halsey, "Commander, they attacked the aircraft carriers because I ordered them to attack the aircraft carriers. Now, could you please explain to me why the hell you thought it was a dumb idea? We're fighting a carrier war, are we not?"

Spike spins around, "Um, uh, I'm sorry, sir."

"That does not answer the question, Commander."

"Um, yes, sir. Sir, those four aircraft carriers are too small to launch or land the F-4s that Japan is flying. The little Zeros and Zekes they're flying against us don't stand a chance, especially now that we all know how to kill them. We had already disabled three out of four carriers. They were not going anywhere. The Marines, though, sir, the Marines really needed our help. Thud and I did what we could, but there were just too many boats. I know a lot of Japanese made it ashore, sir."

Halsey says, "I see. Commander, did you know that three of those four carriers launched the attack on Pearl Harbor?"

"No, sir. Sir, that didn't cross my mind. I have to ask, sir, are we out for revenge or are we trying to win the war?"

"You don't pull your punches, do you, Commander?"

"No, sir, I don't. Even when I should know better."

"You need to work on that. I can't have officers spouting off questioning the chain of command. Do you understand?"

"Yes. Yes, sir, I do."

"Good."

Papa asks, "Sir, do the Marines still control Wake?"

Halsey turns to Holtz, "No, they were outnumbered four to one and didn't last three hours." Looking back at Spike, "Nothing you did mattered. Captain, I want the damage reports up in my office in twenty minutes." He turns on a heel and leaves.

Papa takes a deep breath, "I'll have them right up."

A SMALL FISHING PIER NEAR GOTHENBURG SWEDEN

Captain Louis 'Shotgun' Mossberg, USMC, stands, bundled up in a civilian coat, the collar up against the cold. And it's cold. It's bitter this far north on the Baltic Sea. The wool cap pulled down over his ears helps. He's from the south, damn it, and he's black. This is no place for him. But he can't afford to fidget. Not here. He's a Marine and he's been cold before.

He thinks back on the tortuous path that has led him, a Marine captain on a NATO air base in Germany, to this deserted dock. He barely made it out of Brendenmeyer ahead of the Nazi's. The holes punched in his F/A-18 caused him to leak fuel, and with the four nuclear weapons stored at Brendenmeyer under his wings, it was clear he knew he wouldn't make Britain. Instead, he turned north to Sweden. Two miles off the Swedish coast he ditched his plane, sending the devices to the bottom of the Baltic Sea.

He'd planned to swim to Sweden. If it hadn't been for an old fisherman plucking him out of the icy water, half frozen, he knew his fate would have been with his plane. When ashore he was picked up by the Swedish police. After a few days of interrogation, he was released, but forbidden to leave Sweden. His problem is he knows that Sweden is only technically neutral and there's Nazi agents everywhere. Vigilance is his only defense. Nazis, Jesus Christ, man. He was still trying to take it all in.

Then the crunch of footsteps on snow alerts him to someone approaching. The man stops at the foot of the dock and using cupped hands, lights a cigarette. That's the signal. Mossberg walks to the man, startling him, but he quickly regains his composure. "I didn't see you. I'll say this, you know how to hide in plain sight."

"I wasn't from the best of neighborhoods, man. Can we get this over with?"

"This way." They walk down the pier and step down into a small fishing boat. Silent, they cast off the lines and prepare to get underway. The man moves with experienced efficiency. A small engine starts up and they move away from the pier and out into the harbor. "You can call me Dan. Not my real name, but it'll do."

"I'm Louis Mossberg. It's my real name, because for me, there ain't no point in lying."

"You're an American. How the bloody hell did you end up freezing your arse off in Sweden?"

"It's a long story and one you don't need to know anything about. Just know it's really, really important that I get to Britain."

"Well, you happen to be on the right fishing boat. It'll take a couple of hours, then we'll meet up with the patrol craft and I'll turn you over. After that, you're on your own."

"Yeah, I'm kinda used to that."

BLACK KNIGHT READY ROOM, USS CARL VINSON

0550, 1 February, 1942

As Spike walks into the ready room all eyes turn to her. The pilots and RIOs are already in their gear and ready to be briefed. "Guys, we've been scrubbed from the Marshall Island mission. The staff told me they can't afford the fuel."

Lt. JG Lorne 'Jedi' Luke says, "What the hell, ma'am? What the hell? We're the best fucking pilots on the ship."

"I know. I'm sorry. Swede, could I see you in my office?"

Swede gets up, sharing a knowing look with Gandhi, and follows her into her office.

"I'm sorry, Swede. After Wake Island I mouthed off to Halsey about the carriers and now this. I'm fucking it up for all the guys."

"Boss, whatever the hell is going on upstairs, you did the right thing taking out those boats. Halsey needs to pull his head out of his ass."

"Swede, Halsey is the boss. Whenever you mouth off to the boss, you're wrong. I was wrong. Swede, I'll go apologize to Halsey, maybe I can make things better."

NORTH SEA, 200 MILES EAST OF EDINBURGH

Dan is good to his word. In the small fishing boat, they continue through the night, transiting through the islands at the mouth of the Baltic, and make it to the North Sea. The seas are picking up when a spot light hits them and a distinctly British voice calls out, "Heave too, and prepare to be boarded."

Dan says, "There's no need for that Captain Newby. I do however have a passenger for you."

"I see. Very good, Commander. Now, who do you have for me?"

Mossberg speaks up, "Captain Louis Mossberg, U.S. Marine Corps. Request permission to come aboard."

The light plays over Mossberg. Newby says, "An officer of African descent. I didn't know the yanks were allowing that. All good to me, though. Please, come aboard His Majesty's Destroyer Echo."

Mossberg scrambles up a boarding ladder with his pack on his back. Once on board he salutes the flag on the main mast and then the officer in front of him, "Request to come aboard."

LCDR Cecil Hugo de Boisville Newby, RN, returns the salute, "I'm Lt. Commander Newby, commander of Echo. Please come forward to the wardroom so we can warm you up."

ADMIRAL'S BRIDGE, 07 LEVEL, USS CARL VINSON

EAST OF THE MARSHALL ISLANDS

0610, 1 February, 1942

Spike, still in her flight suit enters the Admiral's bridge saying, "Request to enter the bridge and speak."

Captain Van Zandt, at the admiral's side, says, "Enter."

"Admiral Halsey?"

Halsey is looking over the flight deck as the F-14s, F/A-18s, and A-6s launch. He says, "Yes, Commander."

"Sir, I'm sorry I questioned your judgment at Wake Island. I allowed my emotions to cloud my judgment and I promise you, sir, it will not happen again."

"Are you saying this because you know you were wrong or is it because your pissed off for being written out of the Marshall's attack."

"I was wrong, sir. That said, I don't want my mistake to hurt my guys."

"You know, Commander, this war isn't all about you. You were scrubbed because we need to conserve fuel. You were already told that. I know your squadron has racked up a lot of kills. See to it does not go to your head. Dismissed."

As Spike walks from the bridge, Captain Van Zandt quietly asks, "Sir, could we have saved Wake?"

"I don't know, Captain. Let's focus on what is in front of us."

CHAPTER 11

SUPPLY DEPARTMENT OFFICES, USS CARL VINSON

1400, 2 February, 1942

Lt. JG John 'Gunner' Harden, a tall athletic black man, walks into Lt. Donald Troy's office carrying a pile of flight suits. He places them on the Lieutenant's desk, "Someone in laundry has decided to change my rank, Lieutenant. Can I get my uniforms fixed?"

Troy looks at him quizzically and picks up a flight suit. He finds the collar where the rank should be and sees the needle holes in the fabric where the single silver bar was cut off. Instead, in ink is the word 'nigger'.

Troy's lips tighten, "I see. What stateroom are you in?"

"03-174-4L"

Troy consults a binder, then picks up the phone, "Chief Arpao, I need Seaman Dillard in my office immediately." He hangs up, "Lieutenant, we will fix your uniforms and get them back to you today."

"Thank you, sir."

Dillard knocks and walks in. When he sees Gunner, he smirks.

Lt. Troy shouts, "Seaman, wipe that smirk off your face immediately."

Dillard looks at his commander, surprised.

"Dillard, can you explain the damage to these flight suits?"

Timidly, "Yes, sir."

"Well…"

"Sir…" and glances at Gunner, "It was just a joke."

"Where are you from, Seaman?"

"Steward, Alabama, sir."

"And you transferred here from the Duncan after it sank."

"Yes, sir."

"Explain to Lt. Harden why your little joke was funny."

"Sir?"

"You have disrespected a superior officer, defaced government property, and used hate speech, which is conduct unbecoming. You say it was a joke. Explain it."

Dillard turns to Gunner, "Sir, I grew up in Alabama. I was telling the guys that no white man should ever do laundry for a, um for a nigg…um, someone…a darky. I mean where I'm from it is nig…darkies who do the laundry for us. It isn't disrespect, it's just the plain truth."

Gunner shakes his head, "Seaman, you are from the Jim Crow south. Where and when you grew up it was acceptable to murder a man because of the color of his skin. My own grandfather was hung from a tree in his own front yard by someone like you. All that changed in the 1960's. People like you either learned to behave civilly or rotted in jail. Those people who persist in their prejudice keep silent about it or find themselves on the fringes of society.

"The Navy cannot control what you think, but it can control what you do. In this man's navy, you do not EVER address a black person as nigger. There are some on this ship who would beat you for doing so. I will not because my mother taught me to respect mankind. That is a lesson you'd better take to heart.

"Now, by rights, I could ask the Lieutenant to send you before the Captain. With the Lieutenant, and the SUPPO's permission, I suggest another solution. I, and a number of other black officers, will be served our dinner by you in wardroom 1 tomorrow. Seaman Dillard, you will do so with the utmost respect and dignity, or you will see the Captain." Turning to Troy, "Is that acceptable to you, Lieutenant?"

"It's perfect, Lieutenant." To Dillard, "Before you serve the meal your uniform will be inspected, seaman. If you fail in anyway, it will be the brig and bread and water. Am I clear?"

Shaking, Seaman Dillard says, "Yes, sir."

PIER 3 PUGET SOUND NAVAL SHIPYARD, BREMERTON WASHINGTON

1105, 3 February, 1942

Slowly, the USS San Francisco, CA-38, comes into view. Behind her is the USS Long Beach, CGN-9, with her distinctive box bent forward. Captain Warren, bundled up in his pea coat, notices the workers on the pier slow, then stop and stare at the odd vessel. He says to Lt. Hughes beside him, "She looks a little worse for wear."

"Yes, sir, she does." Shawn is wearing dress pants, a white button up shirt, a heavy wool jacket, and a white hard hat stenciled with the letters NRRO. They stand for Naval Reactors Regional Office. "Captain Tenzar is going to hate what you have to say to him."

Warren sighs, "I know, but it has to be done." Addressing the men and women watching the Long Beach, "Gentlemen. There is work to be done."

The workers touch their hands to their hard hats and get busy. Hughes laughs, "If you'd talked to me like that, I would've mouthed off."

"I know, Shawn, but I didn't have four stripes on my jacket then. It seems to make a difference."

"I wonder who they'll dislike more, you or me? I mean you're bearing bad news, but I'm the dreaded NRRO."

Warren smiles, "I don't want your job. You're good at it, I know, but I wouldn't want it." NRRO are nuclear power program inspectors. They have the power to discipline even the smallest violations of procedures or maintenance. They are important and necessary but reside somewhere below IRS agents in popularity.

They watch the damaged vessel pull in and moor. A crane maneuvers a metal brow into position, as a dark gray navy sedan pulls up. Both men salute as RADM Klindt, RADM Charles S. Freeman, and CDR J.C. Morong climb out of the car. The five officers and several civilian project planners go onboard. Admiral Klindt smiles at his friend, Hughes, and whispers, "Don't forget, you're not supposed to salute."

Captain Tenzar waits for the official party as they salute the flag, then himself, "Naval Reactors arriving. Naval District 13 arriving. Captain, United States Navy, arriving. Naval Yard Puget Sound arriving." Tenzar smiles, "Welcome to USS Long Beach, gentlemen. Sorry, I don't have the wardroom to host you in, but I do have a make-do office."

Hughes asks, "Sir, can you point me to your rad con office? It seems the shipyard is lacking in dosimetry."

Tenzar turns to Klindt, "We have NRRO already? Does he know what he's doing?"

Klindt looks Tenzar square in the eyes, "As I recall, you turned down the job of NAVSEA-08. Are you now telling me how to do it?"

Tenzar looks away and sighs, "No, sir." Turning to Hughes, "Rad con is forward of the enlisted mess second deck starboard side. You'll find my ship and my crew in order."

Shawn smiles, "Yes, sir, I'm sure I will."

WARDROOM 1, USS CARL VINSON

1730, 3 February, 1942

Seaman Dillard walks up to the designated table. Lt. JG Harden sits there with four other black officers. "Good evening, Seaman. I would like a cup of coffee, please, and the meatloaf."

"Yes, sir."

"Thank you."

Lt. Jones from Reactor Dept., says, "I would also like the meatloaf. Could you please get me a Coke?"

"Yes, sir."

"Thank you."

Lt. Lonnie 'Tripod' Guiles of the Tomcatters is next, "Good evening, could I please have two bowls of the beef soup, a salad with ranch, and a cup of coffee?"

"Yes, sir."

"Thank you very much."

Dillard takes the rest of the orders, then fetches their drinks. As he brings them their food, the officers thank him. Later, as he clears their plates, Harden says, "Seaman Dillard, could you please get each of us a bowl of soft serve ice cream, and one for yourself, as well."

Dillard eyes widen, Yes, sir."

As he fills the bowls with the ice cream, he asks the mess decks master at arms, "They told me to get a bowl for me, too. What do I do?"

"You get a bowl for you and join them. It happens."

Seaman Dillard sets a bowl in front of each officer, then one at the empty chair, and sits down. He says a quick prayer and looks up. The officers have started eating, so he takes a bite.

Lt. JG Harden says, "Now, Seaman Dillard, isn't it much better when we all get along?"

"Yes, sir."

"I recognize you have to overcome the worst parts of your upbringing, and that is difficult, but I promise you, if you put in the work, you will be a much better person for it."

"Thank you, sir."

"Gentlemen, Seaman Dillard is from Alabama. I think it is time we got acquainted. And, Seaman Dillard, thank you for our meal."

HANGAR BAY 1, FORWARD, USS CARL VINSON

1800, 3 February, 1942

Sam stands, relaxed and ready, waiting for Gandhi to move on her. He moves in, fast, low, and smooth, reaching for her left hand. She side steps, locks up his right hand, and drops him to his knees. She releases him and steps back with a bow. Over and over they practice, taking turns, until they are both sweating. After an hour of Aikido, they switch to Okinawan karate. They work the kicks, punches, stances, and kata for another hour. "Okay, Gandhi, I'm done. You?"

He laughs, "Me, too. Wow. That was a good work out. You're getting better and better. Sure, you don't want to continue?"

"Gandhi, no. Oh, you're teasing me. Actually, I have a lot to do and I have to go. Thank you. It was great."

"Right on, boss."

BRIDGE, USS CARL VINSON, SYDNEY HARBOR AUSTRALIA

0915, 4 February, 1942

LCDR Hunt watches Swede organizing the Black Knights as they man the rails in their dress white uniforms. She puts the binoculars to her eyes, "Pilot boat is inbound at 320 relative, "Helm, right standard rudder."

"Right standard rudder. No new course given."

She replies, "Very well."

"Passing 280. No new course given."

"Belay passing heads."

"Belay passing heads, aye."

"Helmsman, steady as she goes."

"Steady as she goes, aye. She goes 312, checking 324."

"Very well. Ahead two thirds."

The Lee helm, "Ahead two thirds, aye. Ahead two thirds, ordered and answered."

Lt. Sawyer, her instructor standing next to her, makes eye contact with Captain Johnson and smiles.

Forty-five minutes later, Sam, looking through her binoculars, studies the wharf, "The bow is drifting in. Lee helm, back one third, engine one and two, and ahead one third engine three and four."

"Back one third, engine one and two, and ahead one third, engine three and four." The opposing thrust counters the wind as the ship slowly approaches the pier.

"Rudder amidships. All stop."

"Rudder amidships, aye."

"All stop, aye."

Then she sees the ship drifting just a little too far forward, "All engines back one third."

"All engines back one third, aye." Then the forward movement stops and she starts to drift astern, "All stop."

"All stop, aye."

"Fire messenger lines forward and aft." At the line handling stations, sailors with M-14 rifles fire red rubber balls that pay out light lines behind them as they fly to the wharf. The light lines are used to pull heavier lines that then pull up the mooring lines. The Boatswain of the Watch announces, "Moored. Shift colors." The flag comes down off the mast and up a post at the stern. The Navy Jack, a blue flag with 50 stars is raised on a post on the bow.

Sam, using her binoculars, watches the line handlers on the pier. As she watches, she notices a car with a familiar person standing by it. Her heart skips a beat when she realizes it's Admiral Lee. Then she goes back to watching the line handlers secure the ship.

At her side, Captain Johnson says, "You're doing well, Commander. I didn't do as well in my first attempt."

"Thank you, sir."

KING'S WHARF, ROYAL AUSTRALIAN NAVY BASE, GARDEN ISLAND, NEW SOUTH WALES, AUSTRALIA

1034, 4 February, 1942

Admiral Lee and Admiral Nimitz stand in the bright sunshine watching the Carl Vinson slowly warp into port. He's with a number of American and Australian officers. He can't help but smile at their reaction to her size. Captain Potter, the shipyard commander, says, "Admiral, she's huge. So immense. With those overhangs can our pier even handle her?"

"That's why I had you moor those barges. She's tying up where the barges are and will have no trouble. You know, Captain, I never thought I'd see her again."

"She is a very beautiful ship. Did you once command her?"

Startled out of his musings, he says, "Her, what? Oh, the Carl Vinson? No, but I was the commander of her air group."

USS LONG BEACH, CHIEF'S MESS, 2ND DECK FORWARD

1330, 3 February, 1942

Capt. Warren, along with the other officers, is seated and coffee is poured. Capt. Tenzar lifts a mug, "To survival, gentlemen. So, what do we have planned for this fine vessel?"

Warren says, "Sir, to begin with, we will be stripping the Long Beach of her Mark 10 missile launchers, and other weapon systems, in order to outfit two light cruisers."

Tenzar interrupts, "What? You're going to scrap her? Gentlemen, she still has a lot fighting in her."

Warren lifts his hands, "No, no, sir. Please, sir, let me finish. Long Beach is going to get a one- year refit. She'll be outfitted with 6-inch guns forward and aft, and Mark 41 vertical launchers. We agree, she's going to be indispensable. We want to load her with a couple hundred vertical launch missiles, and guns befitting a light cruiser. Meanwhile, sir, we have a lot to do, and while we're working on Long Beach, your missile systems would be better served at sea."

Tenzar sits back, relaxing, "You had me going there for a minute, sorry. Good. It'll take time to get ready to go into dry dock. I'm sure you know that, Captain."

"Yes, sir. Until then, we can start pulling a lot of stuff off her while she's pier side. Also, sir, we would like you to help us set up a proper nuclear power school here at the shipyard."

Tenzar turns to Klindt, "Who will run it?"

"It will have to be one of your guys. For now, can you help set it up?"

"Yes, sir. And sir, I'm sorry I questioned your judgment concerning NRRO."

"Ed, I know you met Mr. Hughes before. It's really important that he gets the kind of respect NRRO must have. I'm sorry I jumped on you. I know you're going to be crazy busy with all the work on your ship. Are we overloading you and your people by asking you to set up the nuclear power school as well?"

Tenzar straightens up, "Sir, there's a war on. Needs must. In short, sir, you need to get it done and I will get it done."

KING'S WHARF, GARDEN ISLAND

1132, 4 February, 1942

Admiral Nimitz and Admiral Lee are among the official party coming aboard the Vinson. Saluting the flag and quarterdeck watch, he sees Sam in dress whites standing behind the rest. Brought back to the moment by Captain Johnson saying something lost to him, he says, "It's good to be back aboard, Captain." His eyes wander back to

Sam. She is looking elsewhere, and there is a sadness in her eyes he hadn't seen before.

"It's good to have you both back aboard, sirs. Admiral Halsey is expecting you in the flag mess."

"Of course. Captain, how did she do?"

"We got a little banged up, sir, but we left Tokyo Bay burning."

One more glance at Sam, "Good. It's a start. Shall we go then?"

SAMANTHA'S AND GLORIA'S STATEROOM, 03 LEVEL PORT SIDE

1146, 4 February, 1942

Sam walks into her stateroom, thinking. Richard's on board and she needs to talk to him. She needs to tell him everything. She needs to cry, but she just can't. Gloria says, "Hey, moody britches, what's up? We're getting liberty in Sydney. This is going to be an awesome day, so get your ass ready." Gloria is changing from her dress whites into her dress aviation greens.

Sam asks, "No civvies?"

"God, Sam, where is your head? You put it out yourself, 'no civilian clothes in Australia."

"I forgot. What are you doing?"

"We are getting off this grey beasty and having ourselves a beer. Now get out of your whites and into your greens. These fucking white uniforms won't stay clean for five minutes out there. Come on, young lady."

Smiling, she starts changing, "You know, Admiral Lee is aboard."

Gloria, checking her makeup, stops, "Is that's what's wrong? He was your friend."

"Was is the operative word. He saw me there and didn't say a word."

"Ah, and now I understand the funk. Get out of it. He's an admiral now. What would happen if he acted like a kid and rushed over for a chat? Think about it, Sam."

"You're right. Do you suppose Australian beer is as good as they say?"

WOOLWICH DRY DOCK, SYDNEY, NSW, AUSTRLIA

1115, 4 February, 1942

The USS Fife is being slowly backed into the dry dock across the bay from the navy base where the ships are pulled in. Parts of their new bridge can be seen staged near the dock. The pilot is watching from the stern as they pull the 529-foot vessel in to the dock. CDR Wakefield paces from wing to wing, watching with binoculars, "Pilot, I see the lines are fast. Shall I secure engines?"

The pilot, John Barnaby, has been managing docking vessels for three decades. This is the first commanded by a woman, "Not quite, ma'am. Let us back at one third for a bit first. Give the old girl some momentum."

"Back one third."

The Lee helm replies, "Back one third, ordered and answered."

"Very well. Pilot, the bow is drifting south."

"I see it, I know my business, ma'am. Two toots of the horn, please."

She gives the order, and the signal is given. The tug starts to push.

Mr. Barnaby says, "All stop, please, one long toot. And, ma'am, my name is John Barnaby, not pilot."

Wakefield, "All stop. The watch carries out the order. She says, "On a bridge, Mr. Barnaby, we all have titles. We use them for clarity. My title is Captain."

"Yes, um, Captain."

CHAPTER 12

BROUGHAM ST., WOOLLOOMOOLOO, SOUTH OF GARDEN ISLAND

1230, 4 February, 1942

Airman Greg Newburg walks with his friend and mentor, MM1 Oscar Hammond. Ham's still moving slowly but improving. They are going into town with the rest of the airframe and powerplant division. Greg asks, "Ham, is this your first time in Australia?"

Ham turns into a tavern, "It depends on how you count. The last time I was here was 1988, so yeah, this is my first time."

"Ham, you know what I meant."

"Yeah. Come on, Duck, let's grab a beer. Aussie beer is the best."

MARKET STREET, SYDNEY

1235, 4 February, 1942

A short cab ride from the base and Sam and Gloria are dropped off at a drab seeming stone building. Sam grimaces, "This is a classy pub?"

"I asked for a classy place where a lady might get a drink. I figured a cabby would know."

"Okay, in for a dime…" They walk in. The only sign above the door says 'The Blue Rabbit'. When they open the door, they can hear a piano and voices. They are in a hall with several doors and the music is behind a beautifully varnished wood one. Gloria pulls it open and a tall older gentleman in a suit asks, "May I help you?"

Sam answers, "Yes, sir. The cab driver said this would be a decent place where a lady could get a drink."

The gentleman smiles, "Of course, please come in. Welcome to the Blue Rabbit." They enter a large room with soft light from wall sconces reflecting off polished wood walls. The centerpiece is a large wood bar. There are a few people, mostly civilians.

They find an empty table and sit. Gloria says, "It's so weird. I expect everything I see to be in black and white."

"Gloria, the world had color before they invented color photography."

"I know, but tell me, you aren't doing the same. It's like old photos come to life, but in color. This place is beautiful, and I keep expecting Humphry Bogart."

Sam laughs, "You're right. Well, here's looking at you, kid."

A grey-haired man wearing an apron approaches, "Good evening, ladies. What would be your pleasure?"

Gloria smiles, "What kind of beer to you have?"

"We'll have Four X, Victoria's Bitters, and Cascade."

Sam says, "The Four X, I guess. I've heard Australian beer is amazing."

"You've heard right. Two beers, then?"

Sam asks, "First, we have American dollars, but no Australian. Is this a problem?"

"No, ma'am. American will be fine. We're seeing a great many yanks about of late. Are you ladies with MacArthur in the American Army?"

"No, we're off the carrier. Navy."

Gloria says, "We wear green as aviators. Do you serve food as well?"

"We do, though Australia is on the ration. Would you care for our beef Wellington, or would you prefer braised lamb?"

Sam says, "The beef Wellington for me."

"Me, too."

As the waiter leaves, two young men in uniform show up. "Good evening ladies. I couldn't help but catch the yank accents and I thought to myself these poor damsels just might need looking after. I'm Flying Officer Andrew Colbert and my friend is pilot extraordinaire Flight

Lieutenant Rogers. We would be most honored to be at your service."

Sam smiles, "Hello, Flying Officer Colbert, Flight Lieutenant Rogers, I'm Lieutenant Commander Hunt, and my friend is Lieutenant Houlihan, but I don't think we need looking after, thank you."

Colbert cocks his head, "But, ladies, I should be clear. My friend is a war hero. He shot down three huns over north Africa. We are fighter pilots."

Gloria asks, "Over Africa? What are you doing here?"

Rogers finally speaks, "I'm an instructor pilot now. I'm teaching the Yank P-40 Kitty Hawk. War Hawk to you Yanks."

Sam says, "Oh, made by Curtis. I know that one. The Flying Tigers in China fly it, too."

Colbert says, "You're a fan of aircraft? We just have to get you out to see our birds. They are the best thing that flies."

Gloria chuckles, "Um, Flying Officer, you're trying too hard. The P-40 is a decent plane, but it is nowhere near the best fighter of the war. Besides, the pilot matters as much as the plane."

Colbert feigns offense, "You malign our plane. You wound me, dear. Ah, but I must assume it is due to lack of knowledge. Would I but have a chance to educate you."

Sam, solemn, "The P-40 is a good plane, but it lacked high altitude performance. Some issue with the supercharger. My wingman, Thud, would know."

Rogers cocks his head and frowns, "What do you do for the Yank military, ma'am."

"We, Gloria and I, fly the Grumman F-14 Tomcat air superiority fighter. It's the best fighter in the war, though the Japanese F-15's are damn good."

Rogers says, "Okay, I've heard of you. You're the group that roughed up the Nips in the Philippines and Tokyo. I got it right?"

Gloria says, "That's us. Well, our air group did."

Colbert asks, "The yanks let Sheila's fly fighters?"

Sam just smiles and Gloria says, "Yes, the U.S. Navy has come to its senses. We're pretty damn good at it, too."

CAG'S OFFICE, USS CARL VINSON

1440, 4 February, 1942

Admiral Lee knocks and walks into his old office. Captain Holtz looks up, and Lee asks, "Got a moment, Captain?"

"Yes, sir. Always. Care for a cup of coffee?"

Lee gets a cup, looks at it, "Hmm, my old cup. It'll do. Tell me about Tokyo."

"It's all in the report. Had to launch early. We got jumped by F-4's over Tokyo, then the BG was attacked by Harpoon's via '15J's.'"

"Tell me what's not in the report."

"Well, I got hit by a lucky shot from a Zero and left the flight after Tokyo. We lost Chaos, Smooth, Book, Bismark, and Knot Head. What do you mean, Admiral?"

"You included the total kill count for each squadron, but not for each pilot. How did they do? And, in private, call me Rick, Jim."

"You want to know how your protegee did?"

"I want to know about all of them."

Papa pulls out a log book, "Okay, here are the totals. She has 35 kills." He hands Lee the book.

"Okay, I want a copy of this. Damn, Thud and Speedy have 31, good."

"Yeah, terminally shy Thud turns into a tiger in the air. Are you going to make Thud and Spike instructors?"

"I'd love to, but they have nothing to fly yet. What happened to Book?"

"Like the report says, he was shot down fighting the F'15s."

"Are you telling me it all worked out between him and Spike. Too convenient. What happened to Chief White. I know he wasn't in the berthing during GQ."

"I've been sworn to secrecy on that."

"Has she?"

"Don't ask her, Rick. Just don't."

"You know I'm going to find out, Jim. I'm NAVAIR jets. You all work for me."

"I work for Halsey. Bring it up with him. Better yet, Rick, just let it lie."

KINGS WHARF, GARDEN ISLAND

0035, 5 February, 1942

A gray sedan pulls up near the officer's brow. Sam, Gloria, and the two Australian Air Force officers get out. Sam waves her arm at the carrier, "We'll, gentlemen, there she is, the USS Carl Vinson in all her glory."

Rogers says a hushed, "Bloody hell. I didn't know anything that big could float."

A black sedan pulls up and Admiral Lee gets out, takes a step toward the group and hesitates.

Gloria says, "She floats, and she kicks some serious ass. That, boys, is our home."

Colbert asks, pointing to the planes sticking out over the edge of the flight deck, "Which bird is yours, my dear Lieutenant?"

Gloria laughs, "Mine, dear sir, is one of those on the stern. The back of the boat for you land lubbers."

Rogers looks at Sam "And yours?"

Sam says, "Mine is the third up from the back on the elevator. I at least try to remember where I park the...car." She sees Lee, "Gentlemen, would you excuse me."

Lee smiles as she walks up to him, but she does not smile back.

"Walk with me, Samantha."

"It's Samantha now? On the quarterdeck you didn't even look at me."

"It's...it's complicated, Sam. We...I...Samantha, I'm an admiral. I can't go acting unseemly, especially not in 1942."

"Eisenhower shagged his secretary. It's not like we are...Richard, we are friends? I can call you Richard, right?"

"In private. When we're around others...you understand."

"Yes. Nothing has changed there. How are you doing, Rick? How's Washington."

"Washington is crazy. We're trying our best to bring war production up to speed so you guys can get parts, replacements, everything."

"How are you?"

"I'm okay. I miss the boat, the guys. I miss talking to you. Samantha, you are good at making the conversation about me. How are you? What happened over Tokyo?"

"You've read the report, right? It's all in there?"

"No, it isn't. What happened to Chief White? He wasn't in berthing during an attack."

"No, is that what they said? Okay, I kind of asked for that. Rick, it's over. Why is it important? Does the Navy doubt Halsey?"

"No, Samantha. The Navy is fine. I want to know if you are. I smell cover-up."

"You know Book's dead, right?"

"Yes, I know. Are you going to trust me?"

"It isn't that simple. Sam fights to keep from crying, "It's hard to talk about."

They reach the end of the wharf and can see across the bay the muted lights of Sydney, even with a black out. Her tears glint in the star light and Lee moves closer and gently wipes them from her cheeks. "What happened?"

"Book killed Chief White with a knife because...because Chief interrupted Book while he was trying to rape me."

Rick's jaw tightens, but he does not interrupt.

"They called away the attack, so I scrambled up to my plane and flew the mission. If it wasn't for Puck, I would have died up there."

He fishes out a handkerchief and hands it to her.

"Book beat up the doc and the master at arms and flew the mission. If it wasn't for Packs warning us, Book would have killed us. He tried, but the Japanese got him. When I landed, I was a mess."

He puts his hands on her shoulders, then pulls her into his arms. "You're amazing, Samantha. No one could have done what you did. No one."

"I had to, Rick. I couldn't let the guys down."

THE KREMLIN, MOSCOW, USSR

General Kryukov looks over the men sitting around the table. Marshall Vasilevsky, General of the Army Timoshenko, General of the Army Zhukov, and General of the Army Konev all wait for him to speak. These are men he studied under, even served under. "Men, Stalin is dead. I killed him myself. I and my men have come back from your future to rescue the motherland from the Germans and the Americans.

"I will share details later. Right now, I wish to make my orders clear. Each of you will retain command of your units. I will assign an aide to serve as an advisor. These officers know clearly what I want, so I would suggest listening to them. We must crush the Germans, of course, but we must do so as a dagger to the heart and not a hammer to the head. We have been too clumsy and wasteful.

"This was Stalin's fault and not a fault of yours. I know you are loyal to our motherland. You must also be loyal to me. I'm not a tyrant. I am a professional military leader. A professional soldier will listen to his subordinates, and I will listen to you, but any disloyalty will be disciplined.

"Now, I am moving up the 5th Guards tank division to the Moscow front. This is my finest armored division. They will push back the Germans. The Germans have nothing that can harm my tanks and my tanks can destroy Germans at over a mile. Already my helicopters are destroying and disrupting the Germans. I am building more tanks at Nizhny Tagil as fast as I can. In time all of your units will also have these fine tanks. For now, this is what I want…"

ROYAL AIR FORCE BASE, ALCONBURY, HUNTINGDON, ENGLAND

Brigadier General Walter Altman walks out onto the airfield with a British officer, Air Commodore Howe. He had to admit the British were working fast. The SW to NE runway was being reinforced with thick concrete and stretched to 7500 feet and the east west runway was also being lengthened to 6000 feet and reinforced. There were already Wellingtons on the base, but with jets defending Germany, bombing was near suicidal. "These new planes are heavy. Makes you wonder how they fly off ships."

Howe replies, "I was briefed in on how all that came to pass. Yes, extraordinary. It seems the whole vessel is designed to make it so. If they can perform as well as the Jerry scourge, though, I'm all for it. Do you know when they will arrive?"

"Not for some time, I'm afraid. Right now, they're in Sydney for repairs. It seems they tweaked the dragon's tail. Left Tokyo burning." Then the air raid siren sounds. Looking around, he says, "We need to take cover."

Howe says, "If you wish," and the two men walk off the runway. As they do, two aircraft overfly the field. They hear nothing until the planes are on top of them, then a rush of noise, and bombs dropping. Altman dives to the pavement, but Howe stays standing. The entire attack lasts only seconds.

Howe helps Altman to his feet, "There is no sense in ducking. It doesn't do any good and the lads don't like it. Now, let's see the damage."

"Yes, well. Thank you. The German jets are so fast."

"Welcome to the war, General." He shakes his head, surveying the damage, "Yes, well, our boys will clean this up in a jiffy."

FORECASTLE, USS FIFE, WOOLWICH DRY DOCK, SYDNEY, AUSTRALIA

1300, 11 February, 1942

LCDR Brewster Flanagan walks up, salutes, and hands CDR Wakefield an envelope. "She's coming together, ma'am."

She looks back over her ship. Her ship. It takes some getting used to. "Do you know what the delay is on lifting the 01 level, Commander?"

"A snag with the rigging gear. They're sorting it out."

She opens the envelope, "Damn it. Oh, Jesus Christ. Don't I have enough to do?"

"May I inquire?"

"Yes, Commander. Do you happen to have a dress uniform?"

"No, but I could scare one up. I lost all my gear when the Salt Lake City went down. What's happening?"

"It seems we are invited to the Governor's Ball. All commanders and XOs."

Brewster smiles, "It's the way of the Navy, ma'am. Just when you are convinced you are overloaded; they show you just how much more you can bear. Truth, ma'am, you could use a break."

"I know, but the whole group is waiting on me. The war won't stop for a dance." Looking toward the pier, "I see they've started the lift. Good."

CHAPTER 13

EASTERN WASHINGTON STATE, 5 MILES NORTH OF RICHLAND

1305, 11 February, 1942

Captain Scott Richardson walks into his office. As the door closes, it mutes the sounds of construction outside. "My God, it's happening."

His secretary looks up, "Sir?"

"It's okay, Lauri. Less than two months ago, I was at sea. So much has changed."

"Would you like some tea, sir?"

"That would be nice, thank you." He sits in his old-fashioned padded leather swivel chair and stares at the wall.

Lauri brings him his tea and a stack of letters. "These just came in. I'm sorry the mail delivery is so slow here. Richland is the back of beyond."

He shuffles through the letters, "It won't be for long, Lauri. This little river bank is about to be the most important site in the war effort." He pulls a letter from the stack, smiling. It's from LCDR Hunt. God, it seems like a lifetime.

Dear Scott,

Just a quick note to stay in touch. I addressed this to the Navy Department because I have no idea where you are. Please send your address. I've no doubt, though, that you are insanely busy. As one of my instructors once told me, 'don't forget to breath'. I can't discuss battles and such, sorry. I can assure you that Thud and I are okay. I miss the brain trust. It was such an amazing group of people. I hope you are well.

Samantha

Scott smiles and can't stop. He grabs a pen and paper.

"Sir, do you wish me to write a response?

Startled that she's still there, "No, um, this is a private letter. Thank you."

GOVERNOR'S MANSION, SYDNEY

1830,13 February, 1942

Samantha and Stephan get out of the bus with rest of the squadron leaders from Airwing 9. She looks up at the castellated towers, "My God, it's a castle. Why?"

CDR Miller says, "It's just the style. Remember guys, this is high society. Don't get drunk. Only the most senior people are allowed to get drunk in a place like this."

Stephan says, "I'll stay sober, boss. I'm too heavy for you to carry home."

Sam smiles, "I would manage. I'm sure there's a wheel barrow around somewhere." They follow the sound of music to the entrance. Holtz and his chief of staff go first, and Sam and Swede are the last ones. The door man says to Swede, "Sir, this event is for commanders and executive officers. You were not supposed to bring a date."

Sam says, "Hello, sir. I'm the commanding officer of the VF-154, the Black Knights. This is my executive officer, Lt. Swedenborg."

The doorman looks nonplussed, then "Of course," and lets them in.

THE SEAMAN'S SHANTY, VICTORIA ST. WOOLLOOMOOLOO

1835, 13 February, 1942

Newburg and the guys, hearing piano music, walk into The Seaman's Shanty. "Wow, Ham, this place is cool. Are you sure you're okay?"

"Sure, Duck. Just don't pick a fight with someone bigger than you."

Greg laughs, "That covers about everybody."

ADC Gellar says, "Find us a place to sit, guys, and I'll order the first round." AD1 McCrimmon, Duck, Ham, AD2 Cervella, AD3 Gnosis, and AD3 Lori Givens walk further in and find an empty table. As they sit, a guy at a nearby table hollers, "My God, the Yanks have invaded."

Ham gives him a head nod and says, "G'day."

The men at the table chuckle and the sailors settle in. Then Bobby shows up with a tray of beers. "This will quench our thirst. They've food here, so I ordered us all meat pasties."

Cervella says, "Wow, Bobby, thank you. I got the next round then."

Ham asks, "Your AD2 pay raise burning a hole in your pocket?"

Joe replies, "I guess it is. That okay?"

"Fine with me, but I get the next round after. Chief, how did you hear about this place. It's nice."

"One of the yard workers. I asked for a safe and quiet place where a guy could get a beer and a bite."

A guy at the other table moves his chair back, stands, spins it around, and sits astraddle, "You yanks off the big ship on King's wharf?"

Ham says, "Yep, that's us."

"Well then, welcome to Australia, mates. Me and me mates are working on the new dry dock. That is one bloody big ship. What is it?"

Bobby says, "She's the USS Carl Vinson, an aircraft carrier. We're from one of the fighter squadrons on board."

"You the ones gave Tojo a hard time a few weeks ago?"

"Yeah, that's us."

"Well then, mates, let me buy you a round. I'm Diggory Plummer and these blokes are Ty, Travis, and Jesse."

GOVERNOR'S MANSION, SYDNEY

1850, 13 February, 1942

There are a lot of people in the ballroom, nearly all in uniform. It's summer in Australia, so white uniforms prevail. The choker whites of the Americans and Australians prevail, with a sprinkling of blue RAAF and khaki Australian Army uniforms, too. In a corner, Admirals Nimitz, Halsey, and Lee are talking with a group of Australian flag officers and an older gentleman in a tuxedo with a red sash. Captain Holtz joins the conversation.

Sam spots another woman in uniform and walks up to her, holding out her hand, "Samantha Hunt, VF-154. Hi."

CDR Wakefield looks at her, surprised, and takes Sam's hand, "Laura Wakefield, Fife. How are you, Commander?"

"I'm doing okay. You command one of the small ships?"

"Yes, Fife is a destroyer. Spruance class."

"The one that lost its bridge."

"I know who you are. You shot down all those planes."

"Yes."

They are interrupted by an Australian couple, a man in the dark blue Royal Australian Air Force mess uniform with three gold stripes on his sleeves. With him is a beautiful woman in an elegant blue lace evening dress. "Good evening, ladies. Allow me to introduce my wife, Abigail Holmes. I'm Group Captain Howard Holmes."

"Pleased to meet you, Captain Holmes, Mrs. Holmes. I'm Lieutenant Commander Hunt, and this is Commander Wakefield, commanding officer of the Fife."

"A pleasure. You, madam, command a destroyer?"

Laura smiles, "Yes. You seem surprised."

Abigail Holmes says, "I think it's delightful. And what do you do, Lieutenant. Commander Hunt?"

Laura says, "She's the squadron commander of the Black Knights. Commander, what was the number?"

"It's VF-154, a F-14 fighter squadron."

Homes says, "A fighter squadron? Have you any kills?"

Sam looks away, uncomfortable. Laura says, "She has 35 Japanese kills. I was just asking her about them."

"My God, 35 kills. That's amazing. Startling. How do you Yanks count kills?"

With a tight smile, Sam says, "We only count combatant aircraft downed in flight. Most of those were Zeros and they are easy pickings for us. What do you fly, Group Captain?"

"I command Number 6 squadron flying the Avro Anson right now. She's a fine twin engine medium bomber. Steady and reliable, as a lady should be. I've just recently returned from Britain. There I flew the Lancaster for the 460th. What kind of fighter can dispatch a Zero as if it is nothing?"

"I fly the F-14 Tomcat, a multi-engine jet fighter. The Zero is a good plane and the pilots are excellent. It's just outclassed by modern technology."

Abigail says, "Darling, let's get some drinks for our new friends."

"Yes, of course." Holmes motions for one of the waiters. "Is it a Grumman product? If I may be direct, when did the Yanks start letting ladies fly?"

Sam says, "Yes, it is." A waiter brings a tray of champagne flutes. "It has only been the last year or so. Well, it's confusing."

Abigail says, "Dear, could we have her and a few of her pilots out to the house for dinner? You could pick her brain about this new plane then."

"Of course. Do you know how long you have in port?"

"At least a week."

"Well, then, perhaps we could have you and three or four others out for an informal dinner. Whomever you wish. If there are other lady pilots, certainly invite them."

"There is one other in my squadron, and I will, perhaps two of us, and our wingmen. That would be four. Would that be too many?"

Abigail says, "No, that would be wonderful." She hands Sam a card, "our address. Four pm on Friday."

They are interrupted by the tall man in tuxedo and sash walking up with Nimitz, Halsey, and Holtz, "I must meet this supposed female aviator. Hello, I am Governor John Loder, Lord Wakehurst. Welcome to my home. You, madam, would you be this female aviator?"

Sam says, "I am sir. It's a pleasure."

"This is rubbish." Turning to Admiral Nimitz, "Is this your idea of a joke, Admiral?"

Nimitz says, "No, milord, this is Lieutenant Commander Samantha Hunt, commanding officer of the Black Knights squadron. She has 35 Japanese kills."

THE SEAMAN'S SHANTY, WOOLLOOMOOLOO

1925, 13 February, 1942

The Aussies and the American sailors are laughing when MM1 Hammond returns with a round of beers. Duck looks up, grinning, "Ham, tell them about turning the captain red."

"You tell it, Duck. It was you on the bypass."

"I know, Ham, but you tell it better."

Tie, one of the Aussies, "So, you pissed off the old man?"

Ham drinks his beer, "Well, we did that, but because we turned him red, not the other way around. This happened last summer after we got out of a yard period. You see, our skipper on the Stoddert, Commander Douglas, did his engineer tour on our boat. I was a second class then and he was an alright engineer and a damn fine captain, but he was always bragging that he knew the plant better than we did."

Diggory asks, "Was he a captain or a commander?"

"He was a commander, but the guy in charge of a ship is always called captain. It's just a thing. Anyway, we're coming out of the yards, and as always seems to happen, more things were broke than before we went in. So, the control pilot on the auxiliary exhaust augmenter valve was broke. It's the valve that maintains pressure on the DFT."

Again, Diggory asks, "What's a DFT, mate?"

"De-aerating Feed Tank, or what we call De Fucking Tank. It's where the condensate is stripped of air and stored before the feed system pumps it into the boiler. Anyway, the pressure on the de fucking tank is controlled by this broke valve. So, we had Duck up there operating the bypass valve while watching a gauge.

"We reported the problem up the chain and the parts were coming, but the captain still wanted to get underway. So, he does this huge ship-wide dress white inspection. Then, before he changes back into his working uniform, he decides to inspect his new gig."

Duck says, "A gig is what you call a captain's boat."

Ham smiles, "Yep, and the problem was the aux exhaust relief valve outlet is above the captain's gig. So, poor Duck is fighting to control the pressure as we are lighting off some auxiliary equipment, and Duck doesn't shut down on the valve fast enough. No shame, controlling on the bypass is a bitch, but the captain was standing on the deck of his gig in his dress white uniform as a cascade of rusty water rains down on him."

"No!" says Diggory.

They all laugh and Ham takes a drink. "So, pissed off, he steams down into the engine room and I'm the first victim he sees. His face is matching his uniform, "Why the hell did I just get my uniform ruined?' And I answered. "Sir, you know the plant better than we do. We reported the aux exhaust regulating valve was broken and you should know where the relief lifts.'"

Laughing, Chief Gellar says, "Oh my God! What did he say?"

"He said, "You're right, MM1. It was my fault, carry on." And he left."

Duck says, "I thought I was dead."

Ham laughs, "We put together some money to pay for cleaning his uniform, but Douglas refused to accept it. We saved it for a party when we got back."

Tie asks, "So, the captain was caught red-handed."

Duck says, "Yup."

Diggory asks, "He isn't still red, is he?"

Ham looks down, "Guys, we lost him. Captain Douglas went down with the Stoddert."

Diggory Plummer says, "Well mate, let me buy another round so we can properly toast a brave red sea captain."

GOVERNOR'S MANSION, SYDNEY

1930, 13 February, 1942

Governor Loder says, "Preposterous. No woman could outfly a man. I hope you are not thinking of sending us this female to defend Australia. I won't have it. Not for a minute."

Sam stands at attention, her face tight, as Nimitz says, "Milord, if I had a thought of sending you my most successful squadron, it would be Commander Hunt's. As it is, I will be releasing the Blue Diamonds, commanded by Earl Carpenter. Their fighters are also optimized for air to ground."

Loder sputters, "Are you telling me that this woman commands the best squadron on your vessel?"

Holtz says, "Milord, I am telling you that Commander Hunt is, right now, likely the best fighter pilot in the world. I admit to having my doubts in the past, but she has proven herself to me."

Halsey says, "Governor, please allow me to introduce you to Commander Carpenter. He commands the squadron assigned to Australia." He and Nimitz walk the Governor away.

Sam turns to Holtz, "Papa, did you mean what you just said?"

"Yes, but don't let it go to your head. You're a good pilot, Commander and you're learning to be a good leader."

Swede asks, "Papa, why does Halsey hate Spike?"

"He doesn't, Swede. He…Look, do your job and don't sweat the high-level politics. That's my job."

Swede says, "Yes, sir."

OUTSIDE THE SEAMAN'S SHANTY, WOOLLOOMOOLOO

2340, 13 February,1942

Staggering from the bar, very drunk, Diggory says, "Hey, me mates. Let me drive all ya to the base. We're way too tanked to walk."

Ham says, "We're too drunk to drive, too. Can we get a cab?"

Diggory says, "A what mate? Ah, a taxi. Not at this end of town. Yer more likely t'find a fag in a bush then a taxi here."

Duck, confused, "A fag?"

"A cigarette, mate."

Ham says, "You think you can drive?"

"Oiy, I reckon. I'm not as pissed as the rest of you lot. Come on now. Just climb inta my Ford and we'll be off."

HANGER BAY, USS CARL VINSON, GARDEN ISLAND

0010, 14 February, 1942

Sam and Swede are quietly walking among the parked aircraft. Swede asks, "Did you know they were flying off the Blue Diamonds?"

"No, it's the first time I've heard anything about it. It's probably why Nimitz flew out. It reduces our air wing a lot. It looks like they will be flying off a Hawkeye and a prowler as well."

"So, we got our ass kicked by Japan with our full force, and now they're splitting us up and having another go at it. This is stupid, Spike."

"Swede, Papa is right. We need to focus on our job and let the leadership do theirs."

They are interrupted by the sound of singing. Ham, Duck and the guys are making their way through the parked aircraft singing, "Whistle while you work. Hitler is a jerk. Mussolini broke his weenie, now it doesn't work."

Sam stops them, "What's going on guys?"

They look at her weaving and salute. Newburg says, "Ma'am, I've just had the best bloody night of my life, ma'am," and salutes again.

Ham grins, "We found an awesome bar. The Aussies are awesome, ma'am. I'll get us all to bed."

Gellar grins fatuously, "Yes, ma'am. We'll get them to bed."

A master at arms joins them, "Shipmates, you're drunk and disorderly."

Ham, quieter, "We are serenading our commanding officer. What's your problem?"

Sam says, "Master at Arms, they're fine. I'll see them to bed. You can go now." The MAA hesitates, then turns and leaves. "Swede, go find Fluffy. We need a drunk watch on these guys. I'll take Lori to her berthing."

She takes Lori's arm and gently moves her along to the passageway.

CHAPTER 14

ADMIRAL HALSEY'S OFFICE, USS CARL VINSON

1410, 14 February, 1942

Admiral Nimitz joins Halsey in his office, "Okay, Bill, what would you say about the performance of Commander Wakefield? You gave her command of the Fife."

"I did. That ship uses a different type of propulsion system and weapons suite. She did an outstanding job of leading her ship through the aftermath of the attack and saved it. I felt she deserved a chance. She's done well. I've heard no complaints and she's always on station and ready."

"Good, but that leads to another question. If you are comfortable with Commander Wakefield's performance, why are you taking issue with Commander Hunt's performance?"

"Sir?"

"You would never tolerate any other of your officers being treated the way the Governor treated her. You said nothing."

"You didn't either, sir."

"If you think back, I did speak up. But we're talking about you and she is your officer. You were behaving out of character, and I want to know why."

"Yes, sir. Sir, you are aware of what happened to her just before the strike on Japan?"

"Fill in the blanks, Bill."

"Prior to launching the attack, another officer, Lt. Carleton raped her. He was interrupted by a chief and he murdered him. Now, tell me sir, how can her men respect her after she was raped?"

"Do they respect her?"

"I don't know. And sir, there is more. After Wake, she mouthed off to her CAG about me. She's a loose cannon."

"Captain Holtz reported it?"

"No, I overheard it. She questioned my decision to sink the carriers. She said the carriers were irrelevant and we should have hit the invasion fleet instead."

"Why didn't you go after the invasion fleet?"

"Sir, that isn't the point. She had no business mouthing off about decisions her command makes."

"It is relevant, Bill. Why didn't you focus on the invasion fleet? Wake fell, as you recall."

"It would have not mattered what I did, and the carriers were some of those that attacked Pearl."

"My staff has told me differently. So, you can't get over the assault on her, and you overheard a private conversation, and now you do not trust her?"

"Yes, sir."

"Bill, she is the most effective pilot we have. I suggest you figure out how to trust her."

"Yes, sir."

LCDR HUNT'S OFFICE, USS CARL VINSON

1550, 16 February, 1942

Sam is standing CDO under instruction in port, so khakis. Everything is in order on board and she finally gets to her mail. She smiles, there's one from Scott Richardson with his address and a short note. He is busy. It's good to hear from him. One from Lee with the new promotion procedures and dates for her people. That was sent before he got here. She chuckles and picks up the last letter. It's from Margaret Hunt, her grandmother.

Dear Lieutenant Commander Hunt,

I hope this letter finds you well. I recently received a missive from the Department of the Navy informing me that you had come back from some future time to fight our current war. I must say, I am astounded. No doubt you are aware that my oldest is already doing so. The clarion call of battle rings true in this family.

We don't get enough information about the war. We saw the attack on Tokyo on the Movietone news at the pictures. I must assume you were involved. The letter I recently received assured me that you have had a number of kills. It seems a barbaric practice to count how many one has killed, but I suppose it is what we have come to with this war.

I am quite concerned, though, that a woman be placed in such a horrible situation. If you wish to come home, we have no shortage of work to be done on the farm and plenty of attractive young men hereabouts, though many, as I am sure you understand, are off fighting.

If you are determined to stay in the Navy, I understand. Or rather, I'm trying to understand. You look so much like your great grandmother, Melanie. If you are able to visit us, please be assured that you are welcome.

I wish you well.

Margaret Hunt

Smiling, Sam pulls out pen and paper and begins writing. When she is finished, she addresses an envelope, puts the letter in, and sets it aside to be mailed. Then, she looks at her stack of manuals and books for her surface warfare qualification.

Sam sighs, pulls the next book in the stack, grabs her SWO notebook, and starts studying. There is just so much to learn, damn it.

IN A TAXI, WOODS STREET, RAAF BASE, RICHMOND

1552, 20 February, 1942

Thud says, "Wow, Spike. They just let us on the base. They hardly looked at our ID at all."

Sam smiles, "Group Captain Holmes must have told them we were coming. There were plenty of guards. They take their security seriously here."

Gloria says, "They should. We're at war. What are they like?"

"They seem nice. I only just talked with them for a bit. His first name is Howard, but it is 'sir' until he says otherwise."

Swede says, "They wanted to have dinner with us so he could learn more about the jets. The group captain was surprised to meet Spike but seemed to come around quickly. The Governor was an ass."

Spike grins, "The governor wasn't all that bad, Swede. We girls have been dealing with stuff like that our whole lives."

"Well, damn it, it's new to me and it pisses me off."

"Thank you, but no fistfights over our honor, ok?"

The taxi stops, "I believe this is your stop, mates." The one-story house is painted white with a large overhang on a shallow pitched roof. It seems pretty new. As they get out and pay the cabby, Abigail Holmes comes out in a peach colored summer dress. "Please, come in. Howard will be along shortly. He's untangling a control cable issue. Would you like a beer?"

Swede says, "Yes, ma'am. You have a nice place."

Sam says, "Abigail, you met my executive officer, Lieutenant Swedenborg. This is his wingman, Lieutenant JG Gloria Houlihan. This is my wingman, Lieutenant JG Frank Jackson."

Abigail puts out her hand, "It's good to see you again, Lieutenant Swedenborg. Very good to meet you, Lieutenant Hoolihan, Lieutenant Jackson. Welcome to our home." She leads them into the house and hands out beers. "Howard and I have been trying to wrap our head around yank aircraft carriers from the future. So, do tell, do we win in the end?"

Swede says, "Yep. The allies kick Hitler's butt and even Japan eventually surrenders. None of it was easy, though." Thud is walking around looking at the photos on the walls.

Abigail asks, "When did you come from?"

Sam replies, "1990. World War II was a distant memory then. The world was relatively peaceful."

Thud asks, "What kind of plane are you flying here? It looks like an Avian, but the landing gear is wrong."

"It is an Avian. My father's. He taught me to fly when I was 16. He once made a bad landing and had to rebuild the gear." Now, everyone is up and looking at the pictures.

Frank says, "I flew one when I was a kid, too. It was a blast. My first hop, the instructor looped it. After my fourth, she let me loop it. I was walking on clouds for a week."

They hear the front door open. "Darling, I'm back. Those blithering idiots in supply ordered 1/8- inch cable…" He walks into the living room and sees them all around the photo, "Oh, hello, my apologies."

Swede says, "So, your supply corps is no better than ours. Figures."

Sam does the introductions, then Gloria asks Abigail, "How long have you been flying?"

A quick glance at her husband, "From 16 until I married last year. I even did a couple of shows."

Gloria says quietly, "I'd never let a man stop me from flying."

Howard overhears, "There comes a time when a woman should be thinking of family. It's how life works. Besides, with the war on there is no fuel."

Abigail says, "I could always join the Yank navy. These gals seem to be doing okay."

Thud says, "They are way better than okay. I think it's wrong to assume that flying aircraft requires a penis." He stops, turning red. "Sorry, I was saying, my mom is, was, um, I guess will be an amazing pilot."

Howard asks, "Your mother was a pilot? What did she fly?"

Thud says, "Mom owned a Cessna 210. It's a six-person personal aircraft with…well, it won't probably exist until the '50's. She also owns a Pitt S-2. She sold her Avian when I was 17. She also flies my dad's Mustang."

Thud has everyone's attention.

Howard asks, "Your father let her fly? What is a Mustang?"

Thud says, "They will probably never exist now, and that is a shame. They were one of the finest fighter planes to come out of World War II. Even better than the Spitfire, which is an excellent aircraft."

Howard again, "Your father let her fly?"

Thud cocks his head, "I don't know how things are here, but where I'm from in Texas...in Texas, you don't cage an eagle. My mom was born to fly. So was my dad. It was the one thing besides us kids that bound them together. She stopped barnstorming and started instructing when my sisters and I came along because the show circuit was too hard on us. Dad did three tours in Viet Nam as a navy pilot, and she took care of us and flew all the time. I was probably nursing age on my first flight. If you love your wife and want to keep her, let her fly."

Sam says, "Easy, Frank. We're guests."

Thud says to Howard, "Sorry, sir. I guess you hit a sore spot with me."

"You wouldn't let a pregnant woman fly, would you?"

Gloria says, "Heavens no, if she pulled too many G's the baby might be premature, and at that age they're too young to work the peddles."

They laugh and Abigail serves more beer. "I think dinner is ready. Shall we?" She leads the way into the dining room.

After a wonderful meal, Abigail asks, "Frank, how did your parents meet?"

"Dad was flying F-4's for the Screaming Eagles and was assigned to fly in an air show in Waco. He just flew a couple of passes and landed for a static display. The Navy wanted him to show off his North Vietnamese Red Stars.

He had two kills. Mom rocked the air show in her Avian. After she landed, her taxi path took her by him and his bird. He blew her a kiss. She caught it and blew it back. Love and airplanes."

Gloria asks, "Thud, were you conceived in an airplane?"

Thud blushes heavily and Abigail laughs, "Gloria Hoolihan, I would think you're jealous."

She says, "Yep, I am."

BLACK KNIGHTS CO'S OFFICE

0915, 21 February, 1942

Samantha is reading a letter from Shawn:

Dear Samantha,

Well, I did it. I bought the farm. It isn't much of a place, but it's away from my work and the frantic activity that's going on 24/7. They have me preparing the maintenance facilities for you guys out at sea. That's about all I can say.

So, I took what money I had when we came back and what was left of my salary that I had not spent and used it as a down payment on this little 30-acre coastal farm in Gorst, Washington. It's located a few miles west of Bremerton and Port Orchard at the tip of the Sinclair Inlet.

I've been thinking of you a lot, and I was wondering, as I recall, you brought some money back, too. While you're out at sea you can't do anything with it, but if you had some way of getting it to me, I would be willing to invest it for you. I'm working with a boat builder to make something like a LCAC. I think it would be a good investment. Of course, I would put your money wherever you think is best. I would keep your investments separate from mine, because I know that's important. I'd watch over them as if they were my own.

I very much hope all is well. Unfortunately, in my current position with lowly lieutenant bars on my collar, nobody tells me anything. Not my brief, anyway. I know wherever you are, you are kicking ass.

Your friend,

Shawn

She smiles and pulls out pen and paper to reply. In her safe she has a little over $3,000, and she saw a Western Union in town.

CONSTITUTION AVENUE, WASHINGTON, D.C.

1400 local time, 22 FEBRUARY, 1942

Admiral King walks out of the Navy building as a car splashes through slush to the curb. Getting in, he says, "Mr. President." Franklin Delano Roosevelt waves his cigar at him and smiles, "Admiral, why hasn't the Carl Vinson battle group left Sydney?"

"They're almost done, sir. The Fife has been delayed. The wiring of the bridge is proving to be a problem. It seems getting 1942 machines to communicate with 1990 machines is a challenge. Otherwise, the bridge is done and the equipment landed."

"Can the repairs be completed at sea? Winston is getting impatient?"

"Yes, sir, I'll see to it."

"Good, let's get the other squadron, the blue somethings, to their place in North Australia. I'm told the runway is complete."

"It is, sir, but there are no facilities to speak of yet. The barracks, and such, are not done."

"Issue tents. We make do."

"Yes, sir."

"Good. Send Admiral Lee from Australia to Britain. We must get this correct."

"Yes, sir."

"Is the submarine making its way to the Atlantic?"

"Yes, sir. It will pull in at Groton, Connecticut, for supplies, then start hunting U-boats."

"Good. Why is it, do you know, that they assume a submarine is the best tool to destroy other submarines?"

"I'm told, it's the nature of sound, Mr. President. Sir, if I may say so, it was quite brilliant of Admiral Ren to keep knowledge of the submarine to so few."

"I agree. One last thing, Admiral. Those special devices. Winston wants one in England, and I quite agree."

"Yes, sir."

"Next Saturday, you and your wife come out to the house for dinner. You need to take a break."

"Yes, sir. It would be an honor."

"Ah, bullshit, Admiral, it will be dinner. But you could use a rest. That is all."

USS CARL VINSON FLIGHT DECK, LEAVING SYDNEY HARBOR

1500, 25 February, 1942

Sam, having been relieved from OOD, walks out onto the flight deck as the order comes to secure from manning the rails. She joins her squadron as the Vinson comes abreast of the headlands and starts to move in the swell. Turning to AOCS Bond, "I'm going to miss Sydney, Fluffy." She looks over their aircraft, "We need to get the crew's heads back in the game."

"You're right. Do we know where we are going?"

"Yes, the Blue Diamonds fly off today. We're going to England. I don't recall the name of the field we'll be using."

"You know what the English blokes thought of us in 1942? They said, we were over paid, over sexed, and over here."

She smiles, "Well, Fluffy, what are we going to do about it?"

He grins back, "We can't stop the course of true love, ma'am. I'll make it clear our people need to respect our hosts. Put the fear of God in them. You just beat the Krauts, ma'am. I got the easy job."

"Fluffy, the Germans have jets. A NATO airfield in Germany came back like we did. Russia and Britain are being hammered."

"How many birds do the Germans have?"

"At least twenty, probably more. From the pictures I've seen, they have MIG-29's. They probably have other types as well. They sure moved fast after the fall of the Wall to consolidate the German air force, and we're paying for it."

"Damn. The '29 has that look and shoot helmet." He pauses, thoughtful, "That means East German pilots came back, too."

"Yes, and they'll probably be okay with attacking the West. We have a real problem to solve when we get to England."

"Like I said, I have the easy job, Spike."

CHAPTER 15

ROYAL AIR FORCE BASE, ALCONBURY, HUNTINGDON, ENGLAND

1000, 26 February, 1942

Brigadier Walter Altman rides in the back of a sedan moving down the concrete runway. The aircraft hangars for the jets are actually single plane armored and buried revetments. From the air they look like grassy hills. The ordinance bunkers are also disguised. The squadron offices and barracks are being built behind the revetments. He turns to Admiral Lee, "Is this all really necessary? These new aircraft, do they need runways so thick and bomb proof hangars?"

"They need thick runways because they land fast and hard. The bomb proof hangars are there because they are the only fighters England can have. We don't want them destroyed on the ground."

"So, they will work for me? I will have operational and administrative control over the whole unit?"

"No, General. They are a Navy squadron. They work for me."

"You'll be in Washington. I'm the general officer on the ground. They will work for me."

"General, you understand, the squadron is commanded by a woman. She's the best pilot we have."

"Some skirt who thinks she's Amelia Earhart? I'll take care of her for you."

"What do you mean, General?"

"Well, I'm sure you don't want her in command. I'll send her home where she belongs. I've heard they are standing up a female unit for delivering aircraft. Maybe that would be suitable work for her."

"And that, General, is why you will never, ever have administrative or operational control over the squadron. She's an amazing pilot, General, and a good leader. Captain Holtz will have total control. He will coordinate with the British and have autonomous management of his unit.

"General, she's like a daughter to me. Any mistreatment by you, or anyone else, I will take very personally. I brief General Marshall all the time. Do we have an understanding?"

Altman glares at Lee, "We do."

The car parks in one of the hangars. As they get out, an RAF officer approaches and salutes, "Squadron Leader Maugham, sirs. I'm the liaison officer to the air marshal's office. This is James Patterson, the contracting officer for construction. May we show you around?"

FORECASTLE, USS CARL VINSON

1500, 28 February, 1942

'Gunner' Hardin is setting up his keyboard and the amplifiers while he's waiting for Speedy, Too Tall, and Gloria. It's the first time they've been able to practice since Christmas. "Hey, Too Tall, about time. I've just about got it all set up."

"Good. Remember the sound needs to be down. The acoustics in here are such we can take out ears. Too bad we can't turn that into a weapon. I wonder…."

Gloria walks in with Speedy, "Wonder what, Too Tall? Looks like we're all pretty much set up. Shall we?"

They take their positions and Gunner does the sound check. "Sounds good. Let's do it. How about we start with some Patsy Cline, then move on to Barbra Streisand. I think you can carry it, Gloria."

"Okay. I hope I can. Now, one, and two, and three…" And they begin with Walking After Midnight.

O3 LEVEL, CAPTAIN'S CONFERENCE ROOM, USS CARL VINSON

1825, 28 February, 1942

Lt. Jackson leads LCDR Hunt and Captain Holtz to the captain's conference room. When they arrive, Johnson's yeoman motions them in. Captain Johnson is doing paperwork at the head of the table. He hands off some papers to his assistant as they walk in, "Type these up, please. I'll get back to you later." Then he looks at them, "Come in, get a cup of coffee and a cookie, and sit down."

When they are settled, "Okay, Thud, what's this about?"

"Well, sir, I was writing a letter to Lieutenant Severn and I realized something. Japan didn't have any nuclear weapons in 1990, but Russia did. I was thinking, what if an area of Russia came back and they have nukes? Think about Stalin with nukes, sir. So, I mean, we need to have a nuclear detergent to stop them."

Johnson looks at Thud quizzically, "Nuclear detergent?" Then he realizes Sam is struggling to keep a straight face.

Thud turns red, "I mean, deterrent, a nuclear deterrent."

Johnson grins, "Did you write your girlfriend about the nuclear detergent?"

Thud, even redder, "Um, no, I mean, she isn't my girlfriend. I started to, but realized it's too classified to talk about in a letter. That's why I knew we needed to talk to you."

Johnson looks at them, "Do any of you know if we have a nuclear device on board?"

All three nod their heads, and Sam says, "Of course, sir. That's why we had all the security for a few hours in San Diego."

Johnson shakes his head, "That's the problem with security. If we loaded it in with a pallet of potatoes, no one would have a clue. Okay, this is being discussed at the White House level. You are not to discuss anything about nuclear weapons with anyone, especially those from 1942. As for detergent," smiling, "we need to trust our leadership to make the best decision. I want a quiet talk with every '90 crewmember to keep their yap shut. Oh, and thanks, Thud."

Sam says, "Another thing, sir. I have a picture of our battlegroup from the ship's store. It shows a submarine, the USS San Francisco, as part of the battle group. I met the CO and XO in Sydney. Why was it kept from the brain trust?"

"We want to keep knowledge of this submarine and it's capabilities kept secret. That is why those photos were pulled from the store." Johnson sighs, "It's currently transiting to the Atlantic somewhere ahead of us. Now, people, that's a closely held secret. Am I clear?"

In unison, "Yes, sir."

"Good. It's almost dinner time. I think we're having potatoes."

GERMAN MiG-29A, 38,000 FEET ABOVE GERMANY

1110 local time, 1March, 1942

Colonel Henrik Getz surveys his instruments then looks at the clear blue sky. Amazing flying weather and an amazing mission. In his flight are 114 aircraft; 24 MiG-29s, 24 Alpha jets, 28 F-4 Phantom IIs, 26 Tornados, and 12 F-104 Starfighters. His flight, it took some getting used to.

They're returning from a beautiful text book strike on England. Just days ago, Hitler himself gave him the Iron Cross. As a child he used to joke about Hitler. He was ridiculed as a buffoon. But, now, he's met Hitler, and he knows just how wrong he was. What an amazing charismatic leader. Henrik had pledged to do all he could to bring England to its knees and Germany to victory. Hitler listened as Henrik detailed what must be done. Hitler then promoted him to Colonel and gave him command of the jet units.

Coming out of his reverie, "Stone, Hans, tighten up your formation. We're not flying cargo planes."

BRIDGE, USS FIFE, 50 MILES SOUTH OF THE CAPE OF GOOD HOPE

1400, 1March, 1942

Commander Wakefield sits in her chair on the port side of the bridge. It's one story lower than before, but just as large. Canvas walls separate navigation from combat immediately behind the bridge. After a month of training her crew was functioning well. The OOD, Lt. Coats, was boatswains mate a little over a month ago. The conning officer, Lt. JG Potter, came off the destroyer Duncan, and a quarter of her crew was from '42, but they were working together. Even the Petrakis family was alright. She smiles, thinking about a great uncle and nephew on her crew.

Over the speaker, "Conn, sonar, submerged contact bearing 242 at 20,000 yards. Twin screws. Designate contact Sierra 1. Contact is at 100 feet, steering 010, at about 3 knots."

The OOD says, "Very well. Boats, go to general quarters. Call flight quarters to launch Easy Rider 31 and Easy Rider 32." As the familiar gong goes through the ship, he picks up the ship to ship radio, "Carl Vinson, Fife, we have a submerged contact about 10 miles ahead of us. We are launching helo's to prosecute. Do we have friendlies in the area?"

COMBAT, USS CARL VINSON, 20 MILES EAST OF FIFE

LCDR Hunt is standing Tactical Action Officer (TAO) under instruction as the radio call comes in. She picks up the VHS ship to ship radio, "Fife, Vinson, acknowledge contact. We are launching a Viking to support. Stand by on friendlies. Recommend weapons tight until confirmed." Then, "Launch Bird 626." She then looks at Captain Tucker, the RO, and the actual TAO, "Sir, am I right?"

"I'll tell you if you're not. You're doing fine."

BRIDGE, USS FIFE

Wakefield picks up the radio, "Vinson, Fife actual, acknowledge and concur, weapons tight." She changes radio's "Easy Rider flight, Fife actual, weapons tight. Repeat back."

"Fife actual, Easy Rider 31, acknowledge, weapons tight. What do we have?"

She pushes another button, "Combat, give our helo's a steer to Sierra 1 and an update." She gets up and goes back through the curtain to combat.

"Captain off the bridge."

She goes to sonar. They'd just fixed and calibrated their waterfall displays. She's silent, looking over the display chart. She's already in range of the submarine's torpedo's, but it wouldn't be an easy shot, not yet. "It's a World War II submarine submerged, so it knows we're here. Sonar, yankee search." A 'boo waa' sounds through the hull.

SO2 Patricia Hart says, "Confirmed, ma'am. Contact is at 125 feet depth, turning toward us at 4 knots. Ma'am, it's going deeper."

On radio, "Fife, Vinson. We have confirmation from the British Navy in South Africa, there are no friendly submarines within one thousand miles of our position. You are clear to engage."

"Vinson, Fife actual, acknowledge, no friendlies in the area. We are weapons free." She hangs up the radio, "Weapons, do we have a resolution for ASROC?"

"Yes, ma'am," says, GMM3 Thomas, "18000 yards at 240. Weapon is spun up and ready."

She picks up another radio, "All aircraft be advised, Fife will be firing an ASROC at a bearing of 240. Stand clear. Acknowledge."

"Conn, sonar, torpedo in the water. Correction, two torpedoes in the water, bearing 240, range 18,000 yards."

"Fife, Easy Rider 31 is clear of launch."

"Fife, Bird 626 is clear of launch."

"Fife, Easy Rider 32 is clear of launch."

Wakefield says, "Fire ASROC." She pushes a button, "Conn, Captain, left full rudder, ahead flank emergency, come to new course 180."

With a thundering explosion the rocket propelled torpedo lifts into the air. The ship shakes and rolls to the starboard as the rudder puts her hard over and the engine room answers the bells. She asks, "Sonar, are the torpedoes going to miss?"

"Yes, ma'am. If they are unguided, they will pass to the rear."

She picks up the ship to ship. "All surface units, Fife actual, be advised we have two torpedoes passing to our rear. Course is 120 and speed is 35 knots. I do not know the nationality, so cannot estimate range."

COMBAT, USS CARL VINSON

Hunt acknowledges, walks to the NTDS chart, and sees the torpedoes are already charted. She picks up a phone, "Pri-fly, TAO, suspend flight operations immediately for maneuvering."

"Admiral in Combat," and Admiral Halsey walks in.

She changes channels on the phone, "Bridge, TAO, come to new course 210. Come to ahead flank, 25 knots." Switching back to radio, "All units, Vinson, come to new course 210, make your speed 25 knots." She turns to Halsey, "Admiral, we have two torpedoes in the water bearing 265 at 20,000 yards. Flight operations are suspended while maneuvering. Formation is informed. Fife is prosecuting with air support." She picks up a phone and calls Captain Johnson to report.

Halsey says, "Very well, Commander." Then walks to Tucker and whispers, "What is she doing here?"

"She is standing TAO under instruction. It's required for her SWO qualification."

"I can see that. Is it really necessary?"

"Sir, you would have to bring that up with Captain Johnson."

The Admiral turns away, sitting in his designated chair. Captain Johnson walks in.

CONNING ROOM, U-116

Commander Gunther Holbein listens to his torpedoes through the loud boo waa of the destroyer's sonar. "Make our course 195, come to depth 150."

"Yes, Commander."

Lt. Kruse asks, "Our torpedoes? We missed, Captain?"

"Yes, we missed. If we are careful, we may get a stern shot."

Sonar shouts, "Captain. Torpedo close aboard! It just started."

"It will miss, Victor. You cannot hit a submarine with a torpedo. It will pass above."

"Captain! The torpedo has its own sonar!"

"Right full rudder. Engines full power. Dive planes up."

It is way too late. The Mark 46 torpedo acquired the submarine right after hitting the water and tracked it. Programmed to detonate right under the submarine, it dives under and detonates. When it does, the U-boat cracks in half. Every man dies instantly.

COMBAT, USS CARL VINSON

Hunt picks up a phone, "Bridge, TAO, the submarine is sunk and we are clear of the torpedoes. Resume base course and speed." Then, she picks up a radio, "All units, Vinson, resume base course and speed."

Johnson comes up to her, "So, Commander, what have you learned?"

She says, "Training is everything. We practiced this very thing around the table about a dozen times. When it happened, I knew what to do, and in what order."

"Good. At the next training session, I want you to share this with all the other SWO students."

"Yes, sir."

"Why didn't you go to general quarters?"

"Because we were maneuvering well clear, I didn't see the point of causing the disruption."

"I agree. Commander Hunt, Captain Tucker, carry on," and he leaves.

Half an hour later, Hunt turns over to Groovy Miller. As she leaves, Admiral Halsey gets up and follows her out. She stops so he can continue and he motions for her to join him. In the passageway he says, "Walk with me." In a moment, they are in his conference room. "I don't understand you, Commander."

"Sir?"

"Why did you fight with the Governor in Australia? Why can't you be nice?"

She gives him a stunned look, "Sir, I didn't do anything, sir." She braces her shoulders and looks him in the eye, waiting.

"You're a woman. Women know how to win over assholes like the Governor by being nice. Why aren't you nice?" He turns his back and sits in his chair, then spins around and motions, "Have a coffee."

She stays standing, "Sir, what do you mean by nice?"

"Jesus Christ, Commander, nice is nice. Is that a 1990 culture thing? When my wife is around an asshole like the Governor, she has him eating out of her hand in five minutes. Why can't you do that? Why are you so God damned prickly?"

"Sir, I do not like to make assumptions, but, sir, I think you mean this: She starts in with her full southern drawl, "Why Governor," batting her lashes and smiling, her head tilted, "I do declare, I had no idea the gentlemen of Australia had such strong opinions. Please accept my apologies for your discomfort, but sometimes a woman just has to do what's right. Why, my great-grandmother, Melanie, held off a company of Yankee soldiers with a shotgun and two grooms. It runs in the family, you see. I hope you understand." She straightens up, "Is that what you meant, Admiral?"

"God damn, Commander, that was straight out of 'Gone With the Wind'. If you had talked like that, he would have eaten it up."

"Yes, sir, you are right. But, sir, I don't dare. If I use any feminine wiles, I lose the respect, and the loyalty of my people. I would also lose the respect of the command because the assumption would be that I was sleeping my way up the career ladder. That is the absolute truth of being a woman in the military."

"I'll say this Commander, you speak your mind. You may go."

CHAPTER 16

HANGAR BAY 3, USS CARL VINSON, 45 MILES SOUTH WEST OF THE AZORES

1200, 3 March, 1942

Thud and Speedy watch out the open hangar bay door as two large cruisers and three destroyers heave into view. Blinker lights start flashing and Thud says, "Speedy, it's the HMS Ajax and HMS Exeter. These two ships are famous."

"Famous for what?"

"With the Achilles, they sank the battle cruiser Admiral Graf Spee."

Speedy, "Wow. We have a cool escort."

"Yeah, the Brits are doing their part to help us help them. I'm wondering what Britain will be like."

"The Germans are going to be hard to beat. You know they will be good."

Thud, "Yeah," He looks his RIO in the eye, "We have to be better."

CAPTAIN'S CONFERENCE ROOM, USS CARL VINSON

1800, 3 March, 1942

Sam, in undress blues, is ushered into Captain Johnson's conference room. At the table are Captain Johnson, Captain Tucker, Commander Forrester, and Commander David Wetter, the First Lieutenant. They shake hands and Johnson smiles, "Be seated, Commander."

Wetter begins, "You just pulled into Sydney, so I presume you are familiar with the layout. You have been tasked with mooring Carl Vinson starboard side too, as before, but this time we are in sea state 8 with winds from the south east at 75 knots sustained and 100 knot gusts. No more senior officer is available. Bring us in."

Sam says, "Given the sea state, we would be better off assuming a course of 100, rig for rough seas, and ride out the storm."

"You must pull in."

"If there is no more senior officer available, I must see to the safety of the ship. If we run aground, we can lose the entire ship. That must out-weigh any other consideration."

"Good. Explain why the passage would be so dangerous."

Thus, begins dozens of questions from each of the officers, except Johnson. Tucker asks her to take a drop of sea water and explain every step needed to get it into the reactor. Forrester asks convoluted JP-5 system valve line ups and details of how the catapults and arresting engines work. She is even asked what types of ordinance is stored in each of the magazines.

Finally, Johnson speaks, "You are the command duty officer in port, Boston, Massachusetts. Both plants are down with shore power brought on. The XO and I are in DC for a meeting and the ship is in three section duty. You receive a message reporting solid intel that Boston will be attacked by air in the next two to six hours. No idea what type of warhead. What do you do?"

"Do we have the air wing on board?"

"Yes."

"How long have the plants been down?"

"Two days."

Sam pauses and orders her thoughts, "The two highest priorities are getting the crew aboard and getting the propulsion plants up. The plants are limiting. First, I would call the reactor duty officer and tell him we need to emergency sortie. I would authorize setting condition two watches and making both plants ready to answer bells as soon as possible. I would authorize the emergency heat-up rates. As one of my instructors down there said about the reactor control rods: latch 'em, snatch 'em, and pull for Jesus.

"Then I would have the Papa flag hoisted and secure liberty for all hands. I would have the OOD contact the Boston Police Department and explain that we need all the sailors back on the ship. Next, would be a meeting of all duty department heads. Reactor division would be excused. I would tell the department heads I needed a plan to man all underway watches and fight the ship. As they get to work, I would contact shore services to start removing unneeded connections, such as bilge pumping and fresh water.

"As that moves forward, I would contact the port authority for tugs. Once all that is arranged, I would try to contact you and the XO. If I can, I would inform you of my actions and intentions."

"You can't reach us."

"Yes, sir. As sailors show up, if they should bring any civilians, I would authorize them on board and to the aft mess decks pending a solution. I would also accept sailors from any ship in port. We can sort it all out later. As the plants get closer to operating, I would order a muster to establish who is missing. I would contact the other Navy ships in port to determine who is the senior officer afloat. I would ask the Fife and Jarret, who can get underway much faster, to sweep the channel. Regardless of the reactor status, I would use tugs to get us underway as soon as I could. It is a dangerous, but necessary move. Once the engines are on line, we will switch to them. Once clear of land, I would identify the sea room for air operations and launch fighters to defend Boston. Once everything else is managed, I would send a helo to pick up you and the XO."

Johnson smiles, "Well, I'm glad you wouldn't forget us. You are right, the ship and the mission come first." To the board, "Gentlemen, questions?"

Wetter says, "No, sir," and the rest just shake their heads.

Johnson says, "Commander, would you excuse us?"

"Yes, sir," and leaves.

HAVANA, CUBA

2200 Local Time, 4 March, 1942

Ernest Hemingway is drinking with his boat crew in the Floridita bar. Gregorio Fuentes, his skipper, says, "Pappa, they are playing the latest Bogart movie downtown. Let's go."

"Nah, not interested."

"Please, Pappa, it's the Maltese Falcon. It's finally in town."

Hemingway sighs, "Okay, we'll go. But you owe me." He throws down a handful of pesos.

The night is cool and Hemingway takes in a deep breath. They walk to the theatre, its marquee lit up with 'The Maltese Falcon, starring Humphrey Bogart, Peter Lorre, and Mary Astor'. He looks up at the sign, "Hey, Fuentes, maybe it will be good." They go in.

They settle down as the Movietone News begins. It opens with footage of a huge aircraft sitting on the deck of a large aircraft carrier. The plane's engines are roaring with fire from the back and it has no propeller in front. Suddenly, the aircraft is launched into the air, and the narration begins. "The USS Carl Vinson, the most modern military vessel of her time, has traveled back from the year 1990 to our present conflict in order to give us the edge against the forces of Imperial Japan." They see gun footage of bombs dropping onto Japanese Navy ships and aircraft shooting down Japanese fighters.

"Their first attack was in the Philippines, giving General MacArthur the edge against the Japanese invasion fleet. In total, over 300 aircraft, one aircraft carrier, one battleship, six cruisers, nineteen destroys, and other craft are destroyed at the cost of only a few aircraft lost.

"Next, they report to Admiral Nimitz, Commander in Chief of the US Navy in the Pacific, CINCPAC." The footage shows Nimitz and his staff leaving a helicopter and passing through rainbow side boys and Nimitz returning the salute of a navy admiral. "Admiral Ren, in command of the battlegroup from the future, meets Nimitz off the coast of Hawaii, in what has to be an amazing moment. The carrier puts on an airshow to demonstrate the advanced capabilities of these aircraft from the future." Flying down the side of the Vinson are two F-14s on the deck, moving through the speed of sound, vapor flashing on the leading edges of the wings. Then, it shows the dogfight between the F-14's and the F-18's. "The aircraft are F-14 Tomcats and F-18 Hornets. The Tomcats win this time and quickly land aboard." The fighters trap and park their planes.

"Soon the battle group gets its marching orders from Admiral Nimitz and they are joined by other Pacific fleet ships. The orders are attack mainland Japan! The commander of this joint task force is Admiral 'Bull' Halsey, the scourge of the Japanese Navy." Shown is Halsey climbing out of Spike's plane. The camera rotates to show the flags on the left side of the plane. "This pilot has 22 kills over the Philippines. And he can also brag about giving the task force commander a ride.

"And so, off to Japan. When they near the Japanese coast, they are spotted by a Japanese picket boat. It's quickly dispatched, but not before a radio warning is sent to Tojo." The image is one of the heavy cruisers shelling and sinking the boat. "The aircraft launch immediately." Hunt is shown from the back, running to her plane and carrying her helmet and gear. The camera zooms in as Puck helps her with her G-suit and helmet, and they climb into their plane.

Hemingway says to himself softly, "It's a girl. Number 9971211." It's the bureau number of Spike's F-14.

Andres asks, "What!"

"Nothing."

HUNT FARM, STONE MOUNTAIN, TENNESSEE

1012, 5 March, 1942

Margaret Hunt hums to herself as she walks into the kitchen with the mail. She pours a cup of coffee and sits down. The letter in front of her is from Lt. Commander Samantha Hunt.

Dear Mrs. Hunt,

This is difficult. You are my grandmother, yes, but I am older than my own father. There are days I have a hard time wrapping my head around what has happened, and I'm sure you have the same difficulty.

So, I am an officer in the United States Navy, and I am a fighter pilot. I fly the F-14 Tomcat, the best air superiority fighter in the world. Yes, I'm pretty proud of my bird. I have been in a few conflicts so far, but I can't really talk about that. I am alright.

I am also the commanding officer of the Black Knights, VF-154. My squadron is stationed on the aircraft carrier that came back in time. Back in time, that wasn't supposed to happen. It's been tough for my people. In some ways,

I'm doing better than most with the concept, but then, I read a lot of science fiction.

I really don't know where I'll be for the foreseeable future, and even if I did know, I couldn't say. I'm hoping to come visit when they let me. It would be nice to see the farm. It was awhile even in my own time. One thing you need to know, it was tough for you when I joined the Navy. Grandpa and Dad and John supported me. But you and Mom…it was hard for you.

I understand that. It will probably be hard on you now. And I get that. This is something I have to do. I'm in the position of being able to make a difference for all the men fighting out here. I'm good at my job. And yes, I have quite a few Japanese kills. It is a barbaric practice, but as you say, it is what we've come too.

I miss you all. I'm looking forward to seeing you and Grandpa again. I'm hoping to meet Dad out here, even though I'm about ten years older than he. It may be a little awkward. Yes, that's an understatement. Sorry.

I am alright. I have a good command and good friends, and I hope you get to meet them someday. Please, take care of each other. I'll see you when I can.

Love, Samantha

HANGAR DECK, USS CARL VINSON, OFF THE AZORES

1300, 7 March, 1942

Admiral Halsey, Captain Johnson, and Captain Holtz walk toward the Black Knights squadron standing in formation. The air wing yeoman walks behind with a stack of awards. Senior Chief Bond is at the microphone, and LCDR Hunt is in front of her squadron. They are lined up and organized in the order the awards will be handed out.

As they walk out, Halsey says to Johnson, "We're handing out awards for the whole ship. It would be quicker to do just one ceremony for the whole crew and get it over with."

Johnson replies, "Yes, sir, but it would mean standing the crew at attention for about three hours. After an hour no one cares, and by the end, we'd have the opposite effect. If you want, sir, I can do this."

"No, William, they fought for me. I need to do this."

As they approach, AOCS Bond calls, "Ten shun!" and the squadron snaps to attention.

Lt. Commander Hunt salutes, "Black Knight squadron assembled, sir."

Halsey approaches the microphone, "At ease," and the airmen relax. When he realizes the mic isn't going to feedback or blow out anybody's ears, he continues, "You've had a busy few weeks. I'm proud of all of you. We took the fight to the enemy, and you, each of you, fought well.

"Air warfare is strange. In the Army, officers send their men out to fight. With aircraft, the men send their leaders out to do battle. It's similar to armored knights, each knight had squires who cared for their equipment and especially their horse. A knight is nothing without his horse.

"The pilots who lead you, are nothing without their aircraft that you maintain and repair. In a sense, the knight faces the enemy as part of a team. We do the same. We win or lose as a team. We are here to recognize the exceptional performance of some of you, but your success is due to all of you. Hard fought victory is always bitter sweet, because it comes at the cost of friends lost. All of you have done well. I said I was proud of you, and I am.

"Word of your efforts have not remained hidden. President Roosevelt has issued the Presidential Unit Citation to USS Carl Vinson and Air Wing Nine."

There is a stunned silence, they look at each other, then the squadron starts cheering. He lets it wind down, then, "Now to the awards. Senior Chief?"

Bond starts reading, "The following individuals earned an Admiral's Letter of Achievement: Aviation Machinist Mate 2nd class, Joseph Cervella, for superior attention to detail in executing repairs to VF-154 aircraft damaged in battle." Cervella walks up, salutes Admiral Halsey, and accepts the letter in its folder, shaking Halsey's hand. Then he salutes and shakes the hands of Captain Johnson, Captain Holtz, and Lt. Commander Hunt, and returns to his place in formation. Each officer talks briefly to the awardees as they pass. Twenty-four Letters of Achievement are handed out.

Senior Chief takes a drink of water. "The following persons earned an Admiral's Letter of Commendation: Aviation Machinist Mate 1st class Argyll McCrimmon for leading the air frame and power plant division in the repair of eleven F-14 aircraft following the strike on Japan. He expeditiously supervised repairs, including significant battle damage to all aircraft, maintaining six available at all times for sortie, and completed repairs with zero re-work. His conduct sets the example for his subordinates and is in the highest tradition of the United States Navy."

When McCrimmon comes to Hunt, "You earned this, LPO."

Five letters of commendation are awarded, including one to Senior Chief Bond.

He continues, "The following personnel have earned the Silver Life Saving Medal; Airman Greg Newburg and Machinist Mate 1st class Oscar Hammond for exceptional conduct during the sinking of the USS Stoddert by enemy action. MM1 Hammond refused to leave number 2 engine room until all watch standers were accounted for and safely out of the space. Consequently, he received burns to much of his body. Petty Officer Hammond received the Purple Heart during this action.

"Airman Newburg evacuated the five men of his watch team to the weather decks, where he provided aid and stayed with them on the fan tail of the sinking vessel. As the rest of the crew abandoned ship, Airman Newburg stayed with his injured shipmates, attempting to attract a helicopter for rescue. Once aid arrived, he refused to leave the vessel, then in its final moments, until all five were aboard the rescue helicopter. Airman Newburg was also awarded the Purple Heart during this action.

Their quick action, determination, and fearless devotion to duty are in the highest traditions of the United States Navy, signed, Admiral Russell R. Waesche, Commander of the United States Coast Guard."

Bond continues, "Machinist Mate 1st class Oscar Hammond has earned the Bronze Star for quickly responding to the missile attack on USS Carl Vinson despite injuries he received during the sinking of the USS Benjamin Stoddert. He single-handedly put out fires located directly above the number 2 oxygen generation station. Had the fires breached the oxygen area, the resultant explosion would have been catastrophic and could easily have resulted in the loss of the vessel. Petty Officer Hammond's selfless determination saved untold lives. He also received his second Purple Heart for this action." Hammond blushes deeply during the applause and cheering.

"The following personnel have earned the Gold Life Saving Medal: Lt. JG Gloria Hoolihan and Lt.

Commander Samantha Hunt at great risk of life volunteered to act as search and rescue swimmers during the sinking of the USS Benjamin Stoddert. Under the temporary command of Helicopter Squadron Eight, they entered the water multiple times, at night, in shark infested waters, to rescue sailors off the stricken vessel. Their efforts directly accounted for the rescue and recovery of forty-two sailors. Their quick action, determination, and fearless devotion to duty are in the highest traditions of the United States Navy, signed, Admiral Russell R. Waesche, Commander of the United States Coast Guard."

At first there is silence, then the applause and cheering are deafening as Hunt and Hoolihan receive their medals.

After the applause dies down, Senior Chief continues, "All the pilots and radar intercept officers of the Black Knights have earned the Air Medal," and reads off all 22 names alphabetically, ending with Lt. JG Truman 'Johnny' Walker. As their names are called, each officer comes forward and receives the medal from Halsey and Hunt pins it on. Holtz pins hers on. As she pins Thud, he says, "Don't poke me with that," and he grins at her.

Chief Bond continues, "The following personnel have earned the Distinguished Flying Cross for achieving ten or more aerial victories: Lt. JG Hoolihan and Lt. JG Standley, twelve kills; Lt. Harden and Ensign Nelson, fourteen kills; Lt. Boxter, seventeen kills; Lt. Swedenborg and Lt. Jacobs, twenty-three kills; Lt. JG Jackson and Lt.

JG Gonzalez, thirty-one kills; Lt. Commander Hunt and Lt. JG Hawke, thirty-five kills." The hangar bay is once again filled with cheers and applause.

Senior Chief continues, "And, finally, Lt. Commander Samantha Hunt has earned the Surface Warfare Officers pin."

Captain Johnson pins her and says, "You killed the board, Commander. It has been a pleasure to serve with you."

"Thank you, sir. For me as well, to serve with you."

The stunned squadron is quiet, then they cheer their skipper.

CHAPTER 17

HANGER BAY 1, USS CARL VINSON

1000, 8 March, 1942

Puck bench presses 150 lbs. ten times as Sam spots him. "Doing good, Puck. Now, done." He puts the bar on the rack and sits up, takes a breath and gives the bench to Sam. She finishes taking off two ten lb. weights and racks them. Taking a deep breath, she lays on the bench and lifts the bar from its rack.

Ten reps later, its Gloria's turn with G.Q spotting. Sam is breathing hard holding 20 lb. weights at her side while doing squats, then she transitions to lunges. She does them slowly, to compensate for the movement of the ship. She grins at Puck, "Next, planks. I'm glad we're almost done with this session. I've got a ton of paper work on my desk, as usual. Damn it."

They return the weights to their racks and get down on the mat. Planks, push-ups, yoga stretches, squat-thrusts, shot-gun squats, working their abdominals to the max. She grins at Puck as she towels off, "Bet I can do more pull-ups."

"You're on."

They both wrap their hands on the bar at the same time, and begin. Puck counting, "One…two…three…," and on, until at 15 Sam drops off. Puck smiles and keeps going, dropping off at twenty

"Show off. Good work out." She goes to the mat and does cool down stretches; taking her time and letting her muscles ease out and relax.

CAPTAIN'S CONFERENCE ROOM, USS CARL VINSON,

200 MILES SOUTH OF PORTSMOUTH, ENGLAND

1925, 10 March, 1942

Spike and Papa are sitting across from Captain Johnson as Captain Van Zandt and the intel officer brief them in on the war in Britain. Van Zandt says, "The last attack happened yesterday. Over 100 German aircraft hit Portsmouth and London. They hit dry docks and aviation targets. They hit specific military targets and morale targets. They damaged Buckingham Palace. From what I understand, the King and Queen are okay."

Holtz asks, "How is the morale of the people? How are the supplies holding up?"

The intel officer LCDR Guiles, says, "The morale is still high. The harder the Germans push, the tougher the Brits get. They've been rationing for several years. The war department has promised to keep your unit supplied with everything you need. Food, fuel, ammo, and parts as we start making them."

Spike asks, "Most of the parts an F-14 needs are one of a kind. Can we have the locals make them for us?"

Van Zandt answers, "I'll ask Halsey, but it is probably a presidential decision, so for now, no."

Papa asks, "What do you know about the air field at Alconbury?"

"I know the field is freshly paved to our required specs and 7500…Attention on deck."

Halsey walks into the room, "Carry on. Where are we?"

Van Zandt replies, "Fielding questions, sir. It was asked if the British could help make parts and components for the aircraft."

Halsey says, "Absolutely not. That is out of the question. Parts will be shipped once they are available from American sources. That brings me to another thing. Commander Hunt, you have gotten into the habit of speaking your mind. Don't."

Sam's face flushes, and she looks straight ahead.

Halsey continues, "Any requests should be submitted through Captain Holtz and the Army Air Corp liaison officer that has been assigned. I don't need you mouthing off and creating a diplomatic mess."

Her eyes meet Halsey's, and she presses her lips together, staring at him. Johnson and Holtz look at each other, puzzled.

Halsey continues, "You really pissed off the Governor of Australia. I want none of that."

Holtz says, "Sir, I will be the one doing all the outside interactions. It's not like she will dine with the Queen. Our base is out in the hinterlands. It's going to be fine."

Sam silently stares at Halsey.

"Your presence there will attract attention. Just...just keep her away from the press. That is the last thing we need."

Holtz says, "Yes, sir."

Halsey asks, "Any other questions?"

Holtz asks, "Will we be integrated with the British radar net for raid warning?"

"I understand that's the plan, but I do not know the status."

Holtz continues, "You made a good point about the press, sir. Are we able to draw someone from the PAO's office?"

"I can arrange it. I want to be clear, Captain. I want the women out of the lime light. No royal nonsense. Nothing."

Sam's gaze has not wavered, and now Halsey avoids her eyes.

Holtz says, "Sir, I understand. Should Churchill or the King want to meet the squadron, am I to tell them no?"

"Captain, you know what I mean."

"Yes, sir."

Halsey asks, "Any further questions?"

Papa says, "No, sir."

Spike says, "No, sir."

They get up and leave, and Captain Johnson motions for the others to leave as well. "Admiral, a word?"

"Of course, Captain."

"Sir, it seems to me, you are putting Commander Hunt in an impossible situation. You want to keep the leading American ace out of the lime light while she defends our staunchest ally."

"You are aware of what she did after Wake? She has a tendency to mouth off and here if she does so, it could be a disaster. I agree, it's a tight rope, but it seems to me I've no choice."

Johnson regards him for a moment, "As I recall, she never said a word to the Governor. I don't quite understand this situation. Also, sir, do you know why she was so passionate about Wake Island?"

"Does it matter?"

"I believe so, sir. Her father is a Marine. As far as she knew at the time, her father was on Wake Island. Your decision to delay supporting the Marines could have quite easily killed her father."

"Her father would be too old to serve overseas."

"Her father is younger than she is. He's eighteen, sir, and currently at Camp Pendleton in training. I checked, and I told her."

"The time travel thing."

"Yes, sir."

"Thank you for sharing this, good day, Captain."

"Sir, this is my conference room."

FLIGHT DECK, USS CARL VINSON, 100 MILES SOUTH OF PORTSMOUTH

0630, 13 March, 1942

Sam walks out on the deck and AOCS Bond walks up and salutes, shouting over the deck noise, "Ma'am, we're all packed up and ready to off load. I've made sure all the squadron has had the port brief. We're ready to go. It's going to be weird leaving the ship to be stationed in Britain."

"I know, Fluffy, but needs must. Thank you and see you at Alconbury."

He salutes again. She returns it and walks to her bird. Puck has already finished the pre-flight check when she joins him.

A GERMAN AIRFIELD

0730 local time, 13 March, 1942

Colonel Getz walks into the briefing room. One hundred-fourteen air crew are waiting. With them are intelligence and weather people there to brief them in. As he walks to the head of the room, they all stand at attention. He surveys the room, nodding. They are all experienced pilots. It's a shame so few of the other pilots who came back wished to be part of this. They are rotting in prison, and he…he is a decorated war hero. "At ease. Men, today is a historic day. Today we burn the parliament building in London to the ground. Cultural buildings are back on the list."

He pauses as they cheer. "We will break the will of the British. They will be so heartbroken; they will ask us to march in and cheer them up."

Again, they cheer. "So, what do our friends from weather and intelligence have for us?" He sits down in the front.

The weatherman comes forward, "Our submarines report good killing weather coming into the London area today. There will be light clouds at 30,000 feet, but otherwise, it will be clear with unlimited visibility and winds at about

10 knots from the southwest. Further north, it will still be heavy overcast and rain. One thing, it sounds to me like the people of London have a forecast of heavy explosives with frequent showers of lead."

The aviators laugh.

As the weatherman walks away, the intelligence officer puts up pictures, "These are our latest reconnaissance photos over London. We can expect more barrage balloons, as it is the only answer for our jets they seem to have. Newspaper reports are that Churchill has been pleading for help from the Americans. But the Americans are powerless to help. The American aircraft carrier is still in the Pacific and they totally lack the infrastructure to ferry aircraft to here. That said, the primary target, as Herr Colonel stated, is the Parliament buildings."

Getz interrupts, "You said the American carrier is in the Pacific. Do we know exactly where?"

"No, Herr Colonel. We have had no reports of its location since it left Sydney, Australia. Our submarines stationed at the Cape of Good Hope, Cape Horne, and at Egypt have not reported sightings. You told us yourself that it is too big for the Panama Canal. That said, we have no indication it is in the Atlantic."

"They are building a proper airfield in the Fens. They do not do so for nothing. Have any submarines failed to report?"

"The U-116 at Cape Horne is two days overdue, but that is not so unusual given the stormy seas there."

"Or the submarine may be on the bottom and the Americans are approaching. Two days. We should have one more free attack. Tomorrow, if clear weather holds to the south, we will sweep for them. If any of our submarines report a sighting, we must make every effort at sinking it. If we destroy the carrier, they lose their aircraft as well. It is of equal importance to kill the ground crews. As we know, skilled ground crews for jets are hard to come by. Thank you, Major."

BLACK KNIGHTS SQUADRON, AT 40,000 FEET, SOUTH OF EASTERN ENGLAND

0645, 13 March, 1942

The squadron is scattered over the sky in loose deuce formations. As they climb through 40,000 feet, Puck says, "I'm ready to do quick sweeps to see if we're alone up here."

"Yes, go ahead." She wiggles her wings to alert Thud, "Let me know if you need to change course."

"Let's swing right about 20."

"Roger," and she does an easy 20-degree right turn.

"Crap," then on radio, "All units, raid warning. Over 100 aircraft west bound, approaching the channel at 600 knots on the deck." To Spike, "Radar off."

Spike, "Set up a volley, then we'll pounce out of the sun."

"Knights, form line abreast. Come to course 028 and descend. Illuminate and volley on command."

Spike turns onto the designated course as the rest of her squadron form up alongside in a line. Once in place they begin to descend. The dive steepens and their wings fold back as they pick up speed and the Tomcats smoothly break the speed of sound.

Then, Puck, "Illuminate." To Spike, "We have lock." On radio, "Fox one, Fox one."

Spike pickles off two AIM-7s and the rest of the squadron follows suit. Twenty missiles streak toward the German formation.

COLONEL GETZ'S MIG-29, 100 FEET OVER THE ENGLISH CHANNEL

His radar receiver gave a brief blip earlier. He ignored it thinking it scatter from the nearby land-based radar. This time he knows better. He pulls his nose up and releases all the ordinance he is carrying. "Drop bombs and engage." With a quick high G maneuver, he breaks the missile lock, but in his peripheral vision he sees fire balls where once there were aircraft. "Damn, damn, damn. Intel was wrong. The Americans are here."

KNIGHT FLIGHT 12,000 FEET OVER SOUTHEAST ENGLAND

Spike follows her missiles in. There are so many German aircraft. She sees both of her missiles find targets, then meets a third plane, head to head. She rolls on afterburners, pulls the stick back in a reverse, and grunts, "MiG-29, grunt."

Puck, "Thud, right and high."

She sees her opponent crossing her in a vertical scissors, "This guy knows how to fight. Grunt."

"One high, six. Thud has him."

They hear Speedy, "Guns, guns."

She reverses again in the vertical. Her opponent reverses behind them, slowing his craft. "He's trying to burn us out of air speed, where he is strong. Reversing, guns. Grunt."

Puck, "Guns, guns."

She applies full right rudder and idles back her right engine, leaving her left in zone one afterburner. The F-14 whips around outside of controlled flight. As they spin for a brief second the MiG will cross in front of her. She squeezes the trigger right before the MiG crosses. They are so close; she sees the rounds hit as he flashes by. She counters the spin with her right engine up and her left engine back. The F-14 straightens and out of air speed it rolls on its back. She pulls the stick back and dives, accelerating away. "Where is he?"

"He's bugging out, Spike. They are all bugging out. Thud's below us. Do we chase?"

"Not the mission. Regroup."

"All Knights form on us. Check in."

After the squadron checks in, Spike says, "My God, Puck. We didn't lose anybody."

On the radio, "Knight squadron, Gold Eagle. Report."

Puck, "Gold Eagle, Knight 1. We engaged one hundred plus aircraft. We splashed several. No aircraft lost. The enemy has bugged out toward France. We are climbing back up to establish a CAP."

"Knight 1, Gold Eagle, acknowledge. Continue on mission."

COLONEL GETZ OVER WESTERN FRANCE

Getz ponders his situation. He's lost fifteen aircraft in one pass, eighteen overall. Even at their best, he doesn't know if his old squadron would do so well. The pilot he faced was very good. "When I met him, he knew the scissors and didn't hesitate. When I tried to get the him into my envelope he rejected it. How did he turn so fast?" He needed to look into that. He was very, very good. The F-14; he'd faced them before, but never flown as this pilot flew. It changed everything. They may attack us on the ground. So much to do. On the radio, "Keep your eyes alert. They may follow us to our home."

CHAPTER 18

ELECTRONIC DEVELOPMENT CAMPUS, RICHLAND, WASHINGTON

1030, 13 March, 1942

Captain Richardson sits looking out the window of his new office. He's on the fourth floor of a huge manufacturing building designed and built to his standards. The morning sun makes the otherwise dismal view pretty. The dark line in the foreground is the Columbia River. Other than that, all you can see is arid gray and tan with scrub brush. The truck traffic is constant now that things are finally coming together. His assistant, Lauri Talbot, brings in the mail and a cup of tea, "Your mail, sir. Your friend, Commander Hunt, sent you a letter. It's on top."

"Thank you, Lauri."

"Who is she?"

"She's a fighter pilot. She commands the Black Knight squadron. We met on the Carl Vinson."

"There's a woman commanding a fighter squadron? Why isn't that in the news?"

"Right now, the Navy is trying to keep it discrete. It will blow up in the news soon enough."

There's a knock on the door, it opens, and Commander Penelope Severn walks in, "Hi, Captain, nice digs."

"Hi Penny, I just got a letter from Sam."

"Cool beans. How is she?" and she sits down. Lauri pours her a cup of tea. "Thank you, Lauri."

He continues reading, "She is, or was, in Australia. Australia is great. Hmm, she went to a dinner at Government House. Anyway, what can I do for you, Penny?"

"The latest batch of casing material is the wrong alloy. I ordered 17-4PH stainless steel and they sent me copper nickel. I'm just trying to decide if I ought to write a stern memo or throttle someone."

"Is it Kaiser?"

"Yes. I ordered to MIL SPEC, but they sent me the wrong stuff."

"Send the stern letter. I need to head out there tomorrow for some other meetings. I'll give them a little talk as well, perhaps suggesting military orders could go elsewhere. Have you heard from Frank?"

"Yes, he writes now and then. He's getting really good at saying stuff without saying stuff."

"What stuff."

"They're getting low on missiles. I have to get this sorted out."

"You can't ship them until I finish the cards. It'll be awhile. We have a building. I'm waiting for the FABs. They're being built by machine shops all over the country. God knows if it will all fit together."

"Whose idea was it to split manufacturing?"

"The war production board. They're doing it for security reasons. We're just going to have to live with it."

"At least they put our factories on the same campus. My new building is great and it went up fast."

"In another month or so, I should be able to start making silicon wafers. I still need to build a laser that lasts more than ten days. It's going to take time, Penny. Nothing for it. We both know how important it is to get this done. As Admiral Klindt says…"

In unison, "Work the problem, don't be the problem."

ALCONBURY RAF BASE, ENGLAND

1046, 13 March, 1942

Spike and Thud descend over the beautiful green countryside of Cambridgeshire, raindrops streaking their canopies. They flare and land on the new runway. Their tires chirp almost in unison and they slow as they approach the far taxiway. They're directed where to stop, and as their engines spool down, men are pulling hoses from a fuel truck. "Okay, Puck. Potty break." She climbs out of the jet and walks quickly toward a hard shelter. As she nears the open door, she hears more F-14s landing.

The hard shelter is made of concrete and covered in a thick layer of dirt and grass. The interior is spartan, but there is a bathroom against the back wall. Business done; she sees Gloria hobbling toward her. Meeting on the tarmac outside, Gloria salutes, "Permission to pee freely."

Sam returns the salute, smiling, "Go, Gloria. See you in the air." As she walks to her plane, a C-2 Greyhound lands.

Puck is walking around their bird as she returns, "No new holes and we are topped off with fuel. Did we hit the last target?"

"I'm pretty sure, yes, but hard to say. He was good. Yeah."

"I wouldn't think a German from 1990 would fight for Hitler."

"I know, we need to think about that."

The C-2 taxis to a stop near them. All the Black Knights planes are lined up on the tarmac. A-6 Intruders come in to land, two by two. Fluffy walks off the C-2, seeming too muscular for his flight deck uniform. His shouts are lost over the jet noise, but soon sailors are coming out of the cargo plane pulling ordinance. He walks up and salutes, "Ma'am, we just have a handful of missiles, but we'll spread them around. Do you need twenty mike?"

Spike returns his salute, "Yes, I need topping off. We could use two more 7s, too."

"On it, ma'am. We'll have you in the air in a jiffy."

COMBAT, USS FIFE

1050, 20 March, 1942

The XO, LCDR Brewster Flanagan, is sitting in the TAO chair listening to the subdued chatter around him. The carrier is warping into port and the Fife is patrolling near the eastern pass between the Isle of Wight and the mainland. He shakes his head, his last assignment was Chief Engineer on the USS Salt Lake City, a heavy cruiser built in 1929, and today, he's the XO on a destroyer commissioned in 1980. It's hard to wrap his head around sometimes.

Communication announces, "TAO, Bird 621 reports a submerged contact bearing 262. Sir, it's 17 miles ahead of us."

"Very well. ASW start a track."

"TAO, Easy Rider 32 reports a submerged contact bearing 259 at 19 miles."

Flanagan, "ASW, is this the same contact or a new one?"

The ASW plot operator, FC1 Kayla Thompson, says, "A new one, sir."

Flanagan picks up a phone, "Ma'am, we're tracking two plus subs," and hangs up.

"TAO, Sonar, we have screw noises indicating four or more subs. It's all jumbled together and near the surface."

He picks up the radio, "All units, Fife, we are prosecuting multiple submerged contacts to our south and west. Recommend battle group non-ASW units remain in port. Fife is going to general quarters." The alarm sound through the ship.

Commander Wakefield walks in, "Report."

Flanagan says, "Sierra one at 262, at about 15 miles. Sierra two at 259, at about 17 miles. Sonar indicates more contacts."

Wakefield picks up the radio, "Carl Vinson, Fife, can you confirm no friendly submarines in this area?"

"Fife, Vinson, we have zero friendlies in this area. Weapons free at your discretion."

She says, "Tell Bird 621, he is cleared to drop on Sierra one. Tell Easy Rider 32, they are clear to drop on Sierra two. Call Jarrett in the western channel to launch Easy Rider 27 and Easy Rider 28."

A GERMAN AIRFIELD

Colonel Getz climbs from his aircraft. Walking around his craft, he sees three holes in his right wing. So close. So damn close. A car pulls up and a General gets out, "Colonel, what happened? You have returned having lost much of your force."

"We were hit by at least 24 F-14s. The F-14 is a capable plane and they were flown quite expertly. We pushed through, destroying a couple of them. When I judged they had the upper hand, we withdrew. Please understand, Herr General, my pilots are new in type. Until recently none had ever fought in a jet. They are excellent pilots and they will do better as they gain experience."

"How many did we destroy?"

"I don't know, Herr General. No doubt they got the better of us because we were caught unprepared. The American aircraft carrier was not detected. We must prepare another strike. If we destroy their aircraft carrier, we destroy the American effort."

"If twenty-four can maul you, how will you fare against the whole group?"

"Most of the losses came from them jumping us out of the sun. The pilot I fought with had at least 20 Japanese kills. I saw them as I crossed. If you recall, I was concerned about the location of the American carrier. Now we know, and we will not fail."

"I agree, because that was the Japanese. We should do much better."

As they talk, the crews are refueling the aircraft and patching up his ventilated wing.

The General asks, "How many aircraft are on the carrier?"

"I can't be sure, but I would estimate at least 48 fighters, with the rest a mix of other types of aircraft. The Japanese claim to have shot several down."

"Perhaps, but we must assume not, Herr Colonel. What will the carrier do? Will it stay off the coast? Will it drop aircraft and leave? If it leaves, then we need only wait and happy times will continue."

"The Americans would not come this far and only do one raid."

"That is logical, they will leave some planes behind, or maybe the whole airwing. The Fuhrer must be informed. Prepare your next strike. You may use whatever assets you need, but do not proceed without my approval."

Getz salutes, "Yes, Herr General. Heil Hitler."

BIRD 621, S-3 VIKING ORBITING OVER SIERRA 1

Lt. JG Vance 'Splash' Bunton gets the call to drop on the target, "Yes! We get to drop a hot one. Knucklehead, spin up the fish. I'm lining up the shot." AW3 Lewis 'Knucklehead' Baker, the weapons operator, happily complies.

As they circle around into position, the weapons officer, ENS Mike 'Guppy' Tucker, reports, "Weapon is hot. Target is still on course, clear for drop."

Bunton, "Green for drop. Dropping," and pushes the launch button.

Then, ENS Don 'Candy' Kane, his co-pilot, announces on radio, "Drop. Drop. Fish in the water."

The Mark 56 drops from the rail and a small chute opens to slow it as it goes into the water. Once in, the motor starts and the seeker head turns on. In moments, it has acquired its target, the sharp angles of the German submarine showing clear in the sonar. In less than a minute, it closes and explodes immediately below the sub, breaking it in half.

Further south, the torpedo from Easy Rider 32 finds its target and the crews of the surviving subs can hear the rumble clearly as the two subs break apart and sink.

COMBAT, USS FIFE

Commander Wakefield says, "Order the aircraft clear. Do we have a fix for ASROC?"

FC1 Thompson says, "Yes, ma'am. All five missiles are in good order."

Flanagan reports, "The aircraft are clear, ma'am."

"Very well. Sound the salvo alarm. Fire a single ASROC each on Sierra 3 and Sierra 4."

Thompson says, "Yes, ma'am," and pushes the button which rings the warning bell near the forward vertical launcher. She then pushes the fire button, launching one ASROC, turns a switch, and pushes the button again. The two missiles fire, orient to their targets and arc gracefully through the air. About 50 feet above the water, the torpedoes separate from their missiles and drop into the sea.

In the water, their internal sonars turn on and start searching. One acquires its target quickly, shifts from search to target mode, and races in. Diving under the center of the sub, it explodes. The second torpedo, still in search mode when the first detonates, acquires the air bubbles from the explosion and shifts to target mode. As it passes through the bubbles, it loses lock and runs out of fuel. There are still two boats out there.

Sonar announces, "Another confirmed hit, ma'am. The water is so messed up, I can't tell what is out there now."

Flanagan says quietly, "Ma'am, we are getting close."

She says, "Left full rudder, come to new course 175."

At the NTDS with Flanagan, "Okay, Brewster, they were located here, pretty much in a group."

"Yes, ma'am, a pretty good set-up for our assumed departure course."

"I'm pretty sure we've sunk at least two. That will give them pause, but not stop them. The Jarrett is in the west channel and has nothing." She notes the chart, "We have 800 feet and a smooth bottom." Louder, "Sonar, deploy the array. Countermeasures, deploy the Nixie. That should confuse them."

"Combat, radar, we have a probable periscope at 130 relative and eleven miles."

"Do we have course and speed?"

"Ma'am, I think it's Sierra 5. Course is about 100, maybe two knots."

"Very well. Right standard rudder, come to 290. Ahead full. Prepare starboard torpedo tubes."

"Torpedo spun up. Door open. Starboard tubes ready."

"Very well. What is the fuel state of Bird 621?"

"They still have 40 minutes of loiter and they are out of fish."

"Understood. Have them confirm location course and speed. Our wind is about right, let's land our helicopter to refuel and rearm."

A few MAD passes later and the Fife is at ahead 2/3rds, about four miles behind the slowly turning sub. Wakefield, "Fire tube three," and the Mark 56 torpedo launches out of its tube and splashes into the water.

Modern torpedoes do not leave bubbles, so it disappears immediately.

"Combat, sonar, high speed screws at 260 relative and 3,000 yards."

Wakefield orders, "Emergency ahead flank, power limiting." The screws dig in and the ship shakes as it accelerates.

Combat, aft lookout reports two torpedoes inbound at 264."

"Are they going to hit?"

"Aft lookout says they're going to be close. Aft lookout recommends hard turn to port."

"Left full rudder, continue to answer the ordered bell." The ship heels over hard in the turn, and both torpedoes miss, passing astern. One, by no more than 10 feet. "From aft lookout, torpedoes passing astern."

"Very well…"

"Combat, sonar, confirmed hit on Sierra 5. Sierra 5 is hit."

"Very well. Do we have a lock on Sierra 4?"

"Yes, ma'am. 195 at 3000 yards, relative."

"Very well, continue the turn. Come to new course 110, ahead standard. Ready port torpedoes."

"Port torpedo tubes ready, ma'am."

"Very well."

Flanagan, "Ma'am, we're going to run over our array."

"You're right. All stop. Back full emergency. Do we have a good angle for port torpedoes?"

"Yes, ma'am."

"Fire tube two."

"Tube two fired."

"Right full rudder, come to ahead 2/3rds."

"Combat, sonar, we have two more torpedoes in the water, bearing 300 relative."

"Acknowledge, sonar. Ahead full."

"The torpedoes passed astern, ma'am."

"Sierra 4 is hit."

"Come to new course 190 and ahead 2/3rds. Tell the lookouts to search for survivors."

The ship settles on its new course and no more submarines are detected. Wakefield says, "Thank you, LCDR Flanagan for pointing out my error. It's very much appreciated."

"All your training, ma'am. You've been drilling me for weeks now."

"Still, Brewster, thank you. Other than that, did you pick up any errors?"

"It would have been nice if we could have picked them up before we were at knife fight range."

"Diesel boats are hard. When on battery, and at slow speed, they make very little noise."

"Yes, ma'am, I saw that. Ma'am, we sank five submarines."

"You're right. Tell the bridge we'll keep this course for 30 miles, then work a box west of here, 25 miles on a leg. Reel in the Nixie and the tail. Brewster, you have the watch."

She picks up the 1MC, "Good afternoon, Fife. Today we were in a knife fight with five German U-boats. We destroyed all five. I want to compliment all hands for their exceptional efforts. We have done something no other ship has ever done. Boatswain, please paint five more subs on our bridge. Also, we're breaking out the ice cream for after dinner. Thank you, well done."

CHAPTER 19

FISHING BOAT, TOKYO BAY

Lt. JG Chris 'Chaos' Hisakawa focuses on laying out nets as his employer instructs. His life has been difficult since being shot down over Tokyo months ago. He hid in a small cave halfway up a cliff while they searched for him. Then, he watched, in shame, as they found and killed his pilot, his friend.

He waited days for the enemy to give up searching for him, struggling with the cold. When he felt it was safe, he crept out, stole some civilian clothes off a wash line, and buried his uniform. Using the nickname his grandfather gave him, Genzo, he asked for a job on a fishing boat. His Japanese was pretty good. As a kid, his family spent a lot of time visiting relatives in Japan. His grandfather, a fisherman, would take him out on his boat. He'd told the fisherman who hired him that he was a hand on a boat destroyed in the attack. Thank God, his grandpa had schooled him in how to manage nets so long ago.

Haru Satou, his boss, "Genzo, look over there. Have you ever seen a vessel so large as this?" pointing at a ship being built in a dry dock. It was a huge aircraft carrier. Smaller than the Carl Vinson, but still huge.

"No, Kyaputen. I ask, with such large sides how would they handle the nets?"

Haru chuckles, liking that his hand calls him 'Captain'. "That vessel is for carrying aircraft to fight the Americans. It would pull a large net, though. It might even catch enough fish to feed the many hungry mouths inside."

"So, we catch the fish to feed them."

"Of course. Tell me Genzo, why didn't you go to the navy? You handle a boat well."

"They said I was too stupid. All I knew was fish."

"It's my gain, then."

ALCONBURY RAF BASE, ENGLAND

1410, 13 March, 1942

Spike and Puck sit in their fighter on ready 5, waiting. The Redcocks are providing the two CAPs, north and south. With the engines off, it's cold in the cockpit, but at least the canopy is closed. Looking out they see green everywhere on the gently rolling hills. A soft drizzle spots their canopy. Spike says, "What do you think of our new home, Puck?"

"It's wet. That doesn't surprise me. The armored shelters do, though. From the air, they look just like hills."

"I noticed that. The hangars for the Brits over there are normal buildings." A Wellington bomber takes off. All ten birds of the Black Knights are lined up, with their aircrews, ready to launch. Near the hard shelters the Tomcatters are refueling and rearming. The entire air wing, A-6s, EA-6Bs, C-2s, E-2Cs, and S-3s are parked here while the ship is in port. While she's stationery, she can't launch aircraft. "We're going to get some of the S-3s for anti-sub patrols. That will make a huge difference in the Atlantic."

"I heard. We're even getting one E-2C and one EA-6B. Where are all the helicopters?"

"I think they're still on the Vinson. We're supposed to get two."

On radio the British Fighter Command Center says, "Raid warning, north. Approximately 40 air craft over the North Sea. Scramble, scramble, scramble. Rabbit, Jocko, Wagon, scramble to meet the raid." And with that, three British fighter squadrons are ordered airborne.

Then they hear the airborne Hawkeye, "All units, Ghost Rider 333, raid warning north. Beefeater flight 1, steer 018, climb to flight level 35 and engage. Beefeater flight 2, steer 010, climb to flight level 35 and engage. Now scramble all Knight flights. Knight flight 1, steer 180, climb to flight level 40 and proceed at most economical to station Alpha. Knight flight 2, steer 090, climb to flight level 40, and proceed at most economical to station Charley. Knight Flight 3, steer 160, climb to flight level 40, and proceed to station Delta."

Puck acknowledges, they start their engines, and taxi out. Puck, "Alconbury tower, Knight 1 proceeding to runway 24. Request clearance for immediate departure."

"Knight flight 1, 2, and 3, you are cleared for takeoff runway 24. All other traffic, hold."

Spike, "Puck, tell all Knight flights we fly under em-con. No emissions."

Puck, "All Knights, Knight 1. Once airborne, fly emissions tight. Acknowledge."

The Knights RIO's acknowledge. They taxi to the runway, pour on the throttle and rocket into the sky. At 4000 feet, they disappear into the clouds. At 7000 feet, they clear the clouds into bright sunlight. She sets her throttles for 500 knots as the rest of the flight settles into position. On her left wing is Thud and Speedy, on her right is Gunner and NOB. Beyond them, is Glow Rod and Buster.

Puck, "I get that we need to cover the south, but it feels like we're flying in the wrong direction."

"We slapped them real hard this morning. It's Frosty's turn."

Puck, "Fair enough. Station Alpha is twenty miles south of the Isle of Wight. If this soup holds, we'll have to dead reckon it."

"Okay, but they have a bunch of radar stations. We can triangulate off them."

"I have to find them on the map, first. Okay, they use a different symbol, but I think I got it."

35,000 FEET OVER THE NORTH SEA

Frosty leads a four-plane formation approaching the raid. At 40 miles he turns on his radar, "Alright, Beefeaters, we have a formation of 40 aircraft flying at 30,000 feet, at about 400 knots. Weapons tight until we identify. Set your X foils in the attack position."

As they close, Lt. JG Pauline 'Trollop' Cash, flying Beefeater 864, "Tallyho. Angels 30, flying 250. Straight wings. They don't see us."

Frosty, "We have the sun, let's use it. Dive, hit them, and climb out."

FOCKE WULF-190 FIGHTERS OVER THE NORTH SEA

Captain Victor Bauer has his head on a swivel. He's seen how well the jets perform and is not wanting to be caught unawares out here. He knows they are bait for a trap. His FW-190 is a state- of-the-art fighter, but the jets are something else. He also knows if he can shoot down an American jet, he might get to fly one of the new planes.

His first indication of trouble is when his wing man explodes in a ball of fire and a gray jet flashes by. He inverts and dives after the jet, but the F/A-18 is two miles away and climbing again. To himself, "Ah, they slash through like we do against bombers." Keeping his eye on the jet, he pulls back out of the dive and starts a slow climb. Again, the big jet dives on him, and he wrenches into a steeper climb. He picks his prey, his finger touches the fire button, and his aircraft shudders as his guns fire.

He sees some of his rounds hit the aircrafts wing. Then his plane staggers as he feels rounds hitting his plane, and it begins to tumble. He struggles for control, "They use wingmen, too."

BEEFEATER 864, OVER THE NORTH SEA

Lt. JG 'Trollop' Cash shouts over the radio, "Trollop is hit. Trollop is hit. Still flying."

Frosty, "Stay calm, Trollop. Where are you hit?"

"My left wing and engine. Leaking hydraulics. Aileron is fluttering. I need to slow. But I'm still flying."

Frosty, "Trollop, Cookie, fly direct to Alconbury. We'll continue on station."

KNIGHT 1 OVER SOUTHERN ENGLAND

Spike, "Puck, I'm seeing rocks and shoals in Britain."

"What do you mean?' You're not worried about the kids getting into trouble, are you? They're going to be too busy. I doubt they'll have time for trouble."

"Puck, it's no different from a port call. We let them have fun but set the parameters to keep them safe. It's us girls."

"Weren't the Brits more enlightened than team USA back then?"

"I hope so. Okay, we are feet wet. I caught a glimpse of shoreline. The E-2 is way north of us. I'll do a snake, so you can sweep." She wiggles her wings to inform the other aircraft, then takes a one G turn to the west and reverses to the east.

Puck, "Straighten out. Okay, raid warning." On radio, "Raid warning south. We have a large formation 100 miles south of the English coast. They are at flight level 1, at 350 knots. I have visual confirmation. These are fast movers."

"Puck, can Ghost Rider see the flight?"

"No, they are too far north."

"Okay, we don't have time for anyone else. Tell everyone to expedite. We're in."

Puck on radio, "Ghost Rider 333, Knight 1, vector Knight flights 2 and 3 to raid 2. Scramble Felix flights. Expedite."

FLIGHT COMMAND CENTER, RAF BENTLEY PRIORY

Sir Hugh Dowding says, "Launch everything we have in Group 10 and Group 11." A phone talker relays the order.

Dowding asks, "How can this American get visual confirmation at 100 miles?"

John Cunningham, his senior air staff officer says, "Shall we ask, sir?"

Dowding, "Later. I'm quite sure they are too busy to answer right now."

"Sir, we could ask the control center at Alconbury."

"Of course, do so. Also, ask if it is standard procedure to hand control of a fight to an airborne fighter."

KNIGHT 1 SOUTH OF THE ISLE OF WIGHT

"Knight 1, Horne, can you forward pass? The attackers are at the edge of our range."

"Horne, Knight 1, you are not showing up in Link."

"Our NTDS is down."

"Roger, Horne. Fire on 176 actual and we will collect."

The Horne fires two SM-1ER missiles. As the missiles intercept the F-14's radar beam, they turn to ride the beam to target.

"Knight 1, Jarrett, we will be firing for your rightmost aircraft."

"Roger, Jarrett. Buster, they are yours."

The first salvo of missiles makes the turn and streak onto the incoming attackers. The enemy accelerates and takes evasive maneuvers, but at low speed, they are sitting ducks. All three missiles find their targets.

The '14s are moving too fast for a second salvo. Puck, "Splash two. Cease fire, Horne."

Buster, "Splash one. Cease fire, Jarrett."

Now several aircraft are pulling up toward them, though still 40 miles away. Spike, "Fuck, fuck." She realizes she has to take charge. Without Ghost Rider or Horn, they're flying blind.

Puck, "What, Spike?"

She thinks, "Halsey is going to reprimand me. God, my career light is flashing. The guys come first. Halsey can fuck himself."

Puck, "Spike, what is it?"

"Sorry, Puck, I need the radio. Felix 1, Knight 1, put your flights 2 and 3 over Dover. Have them hit the enemy as they leave. Beefeater, let the Brits finish off the prop planes. Make best speed to station Delta and Echo. Felix 1, Knight flight 2 and 3, hit from the north and focus on bombers."

Puck, "No problem, Spike." On radio, "Fox 1, Fox 1."

She fires the two AIM-7's and sees the flare of launches from several enemy aircraft. "Puck, inbound. Grunt." She pulls up, dropping chaff and flares, then whips around to the right, pulling up again sharply, and turning into a yoyo, so she can see her opponents.

Puck, "Low and crossing. Thud's high, left."

On radio, "Knight 1, Felix 1, wilco."

"Knight 1, Beefeater 1, wilco."

She pulls some brief negative Gs as an F-104 Starfighter passes only feet away.

On radio, "Spike, NOB, we are totally defensive. The Tornados are carrying bombs." She rolls and pulls right,

COMBAT, USS CARL VINSON, IN PORTSMOUTH

Halsey asks, "Why are the screens blank?"

Johnson replies, "Ghost Rider is too far north. He can't see the fight."

"So, they are fighting blind?"

"Yes, sir."

Halsey pauses and looks Johnson for a long moment. "Tell them Commander Hunt is in charge."

Johnson picks up a mike, "All units, Gold Eagle actual, Knight 1 is in command. Acknowledge."

They all call in.

KNIGHT 1 IN FUR BALL

Spike, "Grunt," and pulls, breaking right as tracer passes beneath them. She rolls, pulls, "Guns," stitching across the engine of an F-104. It bursts into flame.

Puck, "Guns, guns."

Spike, "Thud, right."

Puck, "Thud, break right, break right."

Thud cranks over his bird, pulling hard Gs.

Spike, "Grunt," as she turns, covering her wingman. Then, "Guns," and squeezes off a burst.

Puck, "Guns, guns," and another F-104 explodes in front of them.

Spike, "Grunt," pulling, as a MiG-29 closes. "Tell Arco and Ghost to orbit over London, Station Bravo."

Puck, "Traffic." She noses down as an F-104 screams by, guns blazing. The high negative Gs sends blood rushing to their heads.

She rolls left and pulls up again, "Grunt." They climb, as again, tracer fire passes beneath them.

Puck, gasping for air, "Arco units, Ghost Rider, orbit Bravo."

Gandhi, "Knight flight 2, volley Fox 1."

Speedy, "Spike, break left."

Gandhi, "Splash two Tornados."

As she whips her plane around, pulling high Gs, Speedy announces, "Got him, Spike. Thud says vertical thatch weave."

Breathing heavily, Spike, "Yes." She pulls the big fighter vertical in the defensive formation.

On radio, Stinky, "Spike, Flight 3 is in. Volley Fox 1."

Puck, "Roger, Stinky."

CHAPTER 20

FIGHTER COMMAND, RAF BENTLEY PRIORY

Turning to Air Marshall Dowding, the phone talker for Alconbury says, "Sir, the F-14 has a long- range camera slaved to their radar to allow for long range identification. Also, Knight 1 is the squadron commander. Lacking other guidance, the squadron commander controls the fight."

Dowding says, "I see. That's sensible. It seems a lot to ask of anyone, though. She must be extraordinary."

KNIGHT 733, AT 3,000 FEET, IN A VERTICAL THATCH WEAVE WITH KNIGHT 626

In Knight 733, Glow Rod and Buster cross right behind Gunner as they climb in the weave. When they roll horizontal, Glow Rod sees an F-4 trying to roll in on Gunner. He tightens his turn, "Gs on." Then fires and hits the F-4. They climb back up, adjusting, as Gunner changes the direction of the weave. The Isle of Wight is getting closer. Gunner dives going for a Tornado flying low over the channel. He hits it and it cartwheels in.

Two Spitfires move in, trying to engage the enemy jets. Buster, "Rod, break, break."

Glow Rod rotates and pulls, tracer fire passing below him. He reverses onto the F-4's six, puts rounds up its tail pipe and another F-4 falls into the channel. Its crew ejects. They invert and see Gunner hunting Tornados below them, and dive down to assist.

KNIGHT 1

Inverted in the weave, Spike notices the German Tornados racing north on the deck. She goes into a dive, closing on the low flying bombers. Puck, "Tone. Volley Fox 1."

She pickles off their last four AIM-7s.

On radio, "Knight 1, Beefeater 1. We are crossing gulf, inbound for Echo. We'll be in your area in 30 mikes, if you need us."

Their plane shudders, and they see tracers fly past their canopy. She pulls up violently, breaking lock on the Tornados below. The missiles bore on, their internal radar holding lock. Then she inverts and Puck re-acquires the enemy on radar. Spike, fighting for breath under the G load, "Beefeater 1, escort tankers. Orbit Bravo."

CAPTAIN HANS KRUGER, GERMAN F-5, ABOVE AND BEHIND KNIGHT 1

Captain Kruger tries to acquire the big F-14 in front of him. Recently transferred from the eastern front, he just knows his F-5 Tiger is the superior plane. Even as the '14 maneuvers, he has no doubts. Three times he has fired upon it, and after the fourth shot, "I hit it. I hit it."

Colonel Getz, on radio, "Did you kill it?"

"Not yet, Herr Colonel."

"Kill it, then celebrate."

As they speak, the'14 moves out of his reticule. He rolls and turns to get back on its six. As it comes into view, it is already inverted and diving towards the bombers below. Again, he inverts, pursuing them. In his single-minded focus, he forgets about the wingman. Tracers go by his cockpit and he feels a huge kick as his aircraft pitches forward out of controlled flight. Nearly blacking out, he manages to reach the ejection handle.

KNIGHT 1, 20 MILES SOUTH OF THE ISLE OF WIGHT

Two of four AIM-7s hit the Tornados. With Thud's missiles, they've managed four Tornados shot down. Some of the enemy bombers are bugging out, but some are still boring in. Spike hears Speedy, "You're clear, Spike. Were you hit?"

Puck, "Yes, but we're flying fine. We have to get those bombers."

Speedy, "You should go home, Puck. Go home."

Puck, "They hit the carrier, we have no home."

They continue chasing two Tornados flying loose deuce, then dive on them. Puck, "Six high. Break, Thud." They climb, roll, then pull horizontal as two F-4s overshoot. Puck "Fox 2," and Spike triggers off an AIM-9 heat seeker.

Speedy makes the same call, and two missiles twist in the air, chasing the enemy planes. They both hit, and the two enemy fighters pitch down and crash into the channel.

Puck, "High right."

Tracer flashes by ahead of them. Spike, "Grunt," then rolls and cranks on the Gs, her wing tip barely missing the waves. She rolls level, "Grunt," then pulls into a violent climb to engage a F-104. As she turns, a Spitfire stitches it with all four .303 caliber machine guns, causing the jet to explode.

FELIX 1, 100 MILES SOUTH OF ALCONBURY, CLIMBING THROUGH 35,000 FEET

Groovy, "Bubba, tell Spike we're 5 minutes out."

Lt. JG John 'Bubba' McInish, his RIO, "Knight 1 Felix 1, five mikes out."

Puck, "Groovy, direct to Dover. Hit them on the way out. They'll be bingo fuel."

Bubba acknowledges, and Groovy says, "Bubba, she's one smart cookie. If we force them into afterburner, half of them will never make it. Tell flight one to come abreast."

Bubba, "Fuck, boss. It ain't fair. The Knights are getting all the luck."

"We'll get a few, Bubba. My guess, half of Spikes squadron will be gone in a month. They're damn good, especially Spike, but war has an arithmetic about it. I wish her the best and you should, too."

BEEFEATER 864, NEAR RAF ALCONBURY

Lt. JG Pauline 'Trollop' Cash fights to keep her F/A-18 in stable flight. She had to pull the fire extinguisher on her number one engine, and the slat on her left wing extended, forcing her to slow down. Her wingman, Lt. Don 'Cookie' Munster, in Beefeater 519, says, "Hey, Trollop, the holes in your left wing and aft fuselage look pretty bad. How's it flying?"

"It wants to pull left. I can keep straight with rudder as long as it's under 350 knots."

"Okay, Trollop, you land first. I'll follow you down."

COMBAT, USS HORNE, 25 MILES SOUTHEAST OF THE ISLE OF WIGHT

The Horne's CO, Captain Aaron Grey, watches the screens. IFF indicates two enemy fighters approaching, followed by a friendly. He picks up a phone, "XO, can you confirm the hostiles at 040?"

"Yes, sir, two hostiles and a friendly."

Grey switches to radio, "US aircraft south of Horne, climb now." When he sees the F-14's altitude change, he says, "Fire missiles." Two SM-1 standard missiles shoot off the bow launching rail of the Horne.

KNIGHT 212, 20 MILES SOUTH OF HORNE

Thud zooms clear of the F-4s, "Where is Spike, Speedy?" As they roll back in, they see a F-4 explode. The wingman pulls up into Thud's sights. A short burst and the Phantom explodes.

Speedy on radio, "Splash one." To Thud, "I lost her a while ago. It's been loco, compadre."

"Okay, call her."

"Puck, Speedy, where are you, amigo?"

"We're over the Isle of Wight chasing Tornados. The fight is scattered."

"The Horne just got our last one. We're turning north, coming your way."

Puck, "All Knights close on Portsmouth if able. We are feet dry southwest of Portsmouth."

COLONEL GETZ'S MiG-29, 8000 FEET OVER THE ISLE OF WIGHT

Getz see F-14s below. He turns and fires two heat-seeking missiles as soon as he has tone. One missile fails to track. One '14 fires chaff and flares and climbs violently, and the second missile misses. He takes a snap shot at the passing plane as they meet head to head, misses and switches his focus to another. It's in a high-speed horizontal turn going after a Tornado. He orients, waits until he has tone for several seconds and fires a missile.

KNIGHT 894, 600 FEET OVER THE ISLE OF WIGHT

As she is turning to reacquire the Tornados, GQ shouts, "Incoming! Pull!"

Gloria rolls level and pulls the stick back, adding afterburner, and firing off chaff and flares. "Gs." A 9 G pull, and the missile explodes behind them. Now, she's meeting the MiG. She rudders a bit and fires the 20mm cannon. The MiG flashes by, "Gs, rolling over the top."

KNIGHT 733, 800 FEET AND APPROACHING THE ISLE OF WIGHT

Glow Rod hears the growl of an AIM-9 Sidewinder that has acquired a target. He pushes the button, firing it off, and it tracks into the right tail pipe of a German Tornado. The engine explodes and the plane pitches forward and sideways, spins onto it's back and explodes on the shore line. The Tornado's wingman jettisons his bombs and turns south, running from the F-14s.

Buster, "Rod, MiG on our ass. Do something."

Glow Rod pulls up, firing chaff and flares, then inverts as he starts a yoyo. As he turns, he sees a missile coming straight for them. He does the only thing left to do and turns harder, trying to break lock. The missile detonates between the engines near the intakes. The aircraft bucks in the air and a slew of warning lights start flashing. Glow Rod pushes his stick forward to take off the Gs and rolls his aircraft to bring it to level flight, "We're on fire."

Buster, "We're hit. Knight 733 is hit. On fire…"

The MiG comes around and fires a machine gun burst at the doomed '14. The rounds penetrate the cockpit, killing Glow Rod and Buster as they eject. The plane crashes in a farmer's field.

KURT WELTER'S MiG-29

The American was stupid. No plane can do what his beautiful jet can at low speeds. If only his wingman would make the same mistake. They make a series of horizontal scissors maneuvers, but so far, the pilot of the F-14 has made no mistakes, and these maneuvers eat up fuel. He calls on the radio, "Schwarzer, Flug, Schwarze Sechs, I am bingo fuel. I return to base, now."

Getz, "Damn it. Acknowledge, Black 6. Return to base. All aircraft check fuel state."

KNIGHT 894, 200 FEET OVER THE ISLE OF WIGHT

The battle is scattered all over the place. Hot Pants is still with her wingman, Swede. "Crap, Byron, they have barrage balloons up. They are firing ack-ack. Call them."

GQ, "Gold Eagle, Knight 894, could you relay to anti-air artillery that they are firing on friendlies?"

"Knight 894, Gold Eagle, roger."

GQ, "Break right. Break right." As they turn, a F-104, crossing above them fires a burst that hits the side of their craft. Hot Pants pulls into a tight turn and rolls on the afterburners. As she does, the plane pulls violently toward the ground and their right engine fans shatter. She rolls back power on the left engine and brings the plane to level flight just above the tree tops.

GQ "Hot Pants and GQ hit. We've lost an engine. He's circling around."

Gandhi, "Brother Swede is on the way. Guns, guns." The F-104 lights up the sky when it's hit by Swede's cannon fire, and the pilot ejects.

Hot Pants starts a slow climb, bringing the left engine slowly up in rpms. They clear the channel between the island and the mainland at about 600 feet. "Fire indicator on our right engine. I've pulled the extinguisher. GQ, we may need to find a place to park."

"Do we need to leave?"

"Not yet. As long as I can control it, I want to save the bird."

"Sister Gloria, if anyone can do it, you can." They make it to 1000 feet, when ack-ack starts up again.

GQ, "Fuck me, not again." A round of ack-ack hits close enough, their left engine flames out.

Hot Pants, "Flame out. No time. We're going in."

On radio they hear Gandhi, "Cease fire, cease fire. Friendly fire west of Portsmouth."

Hot Pants looks out the cockpit, desperately hoping there's a road that will take their big, heavy aircraft. Then she sees a road ahead and to the left. She banks slightly, drops her landing gear, and screams onto the road. She's going 125 knots on a gravel road with shrubs whipping against the underside of her wings. She eases the brake, holding the nose up. If the nose wheel goes down too soon, it's all over. It'll dig in and flip the bird. All her skill and training are being tested in this moment. "Please, God. Please, God."

The '14 is designed for rough landings, but not this. They slow to 75 knots as a tractor comes toward them in a field. The farmer stops and ducks, as a wing passes over his head. Her speed finally drops enough and she gently lets the nose down. The wheel grabs, but doesn't dig in. She manages to bring it to a stop just as the road starts to bend.

Gloria takes a deep breath and takes her hand off the stick. Her hand is shaking uncontrollably. Putting her hands out, she watches them dance in the air. "Byron, open the canopy. I can't. Thanks."

He opens the canopy and cold air rushes in. "Damn, boss. Let's not do that again. Good job. I thought it was all over when the nose wheel came down. Damn fine flying…and driving. You rock."

"Thank you, Byron. You know I can't do what I do without you. Your confidence in me, well…I had to get it right…Oh, my God, we made it."

They're down about a mile south of Brockenhurst, England.

COLONEL GETZ'S MiG-29, 8000 FEET, 25 MILES EAST OF THE ISLE OF WIGHT

"All units, straggle home. Conserve fuel by slow climb at most economical. Report in." More than half of his Tornados, F-4s, and F-104s are gone.

At 10,000 feet and 10 miles south of Dover, his threat warning activates. "Incoming." He goes back to afterburner and turns into the attack. Two missiles are inbound. He violently pulls up, hitting chaff and flares, and the missiles pass behind him. He rolls on his side, turning, as two F-14's streak by. They continue in their dive toward F-104s below.

Returning to base course, he cuts off the afterburner. As he slows, he cusses to himself, "Am I a brand-new cadet? Of course, they ambush us. I am a fool."

CHAPTER 21

KNIGHT 1

Spike overflies Gloria's plane and waggles her wings. "Puck, fuel state and where is Ghost Rider?"

Puck, "All Knight flights, check fuel state and report. Ghost Rider 333, what is your location?"

"Knight 1, Ghost Rider 333, we are over London. We have a good picture now."

On radio, "Felix, Tripod, splash two. Woo-hoo!"

"Felix, Bubba, splash one. Boss says keep it cool and watch your fuel."

"Dirty and Moses are hit. Dirty and Moses are hit. Still flying."

"Moses, Bubba, boss says fly direct to Alconbury. Tripod, escort him."

Bubba, "Felix units form on me. Check fuel."

"All units, Gold Eagle actual, good job. The Eagle is now underway and will recover aircraft as soon as we can. Again, good job. We are proud of all of you. Knight 1, report."

"Gold Eagle, Knight 1, we have one bird lost, one bird made an emergency landing, several birds banged up. We are bingo fuel and returning to base."

"Roger, Knight 1. Felix can handle the CAP for the time being. We bloodied them bad. You and your crew get some rest. You'll have the load soon enough."

"Roger, Gold Eagle. Knight squadron tank if needed and return to base."

As they climb north, Puck, "Let's have Thud check us out. I don't like that shake."

"Okay, flat and level."

"Speedy, Puck, can you give us the once around?"

"Puck, Speedy, you have hits on right elevator, right rudder, and aft hull. The supersonic run peeled back the skin. How does it feel?"

Spike, "Tell him it's a little sloppy."

"Spike, Bubba for Groovy, what are your losses?"

Puck, "One shot down, one damaged and landed on a road. Several damaged but flying."

"Roger, Groovy says we'll leave you Felix 303 behind to bring you up to the ten aircraft we promised Churchill."

Puck, "Groovy, Puck for Spike. Much obliged. Thank you."

GERMAN AIRFIELD

1752 local time, 13 March, 1942

Colonel Getz approaches the pattern to land, "Schwarze, descend to 500 feet and enter the downwind leg." He turns, descending.

"Schwarze, acknowledge."

"Un, Control, Schwarze, descending in pattern."

He lands and taxis to his shelter. There he sees the general step from a car. When he's on the tarmac, he salutes, "Good evening, Herr General."

"Is it a good evening, Herr Colonel?"

"It's been a difficult one, Herr General. We lost aircraft, but we killed many. I am pretty certain at least one Tornado broke through their defenses, but I do not have a damage report from Portsmouth. Many of our planes ran out of fuel and landed in France. We must ferry fuel to them immediately. On the ground, they are vulnerable."

"Of course, Herr Colonel. I shall accompany you to your control center."

ALCONBURY RAF BASE

1655, 13 March, 1942

Spike's plane is the last to land. "Puck, I'm sorry for all the radio chatter. I couldn't figure out how to pass what needed to be said through you succinctly."

"It's fine, Spike. We kicked some real ass up there. You were amazing."

"You did great, too."

KNIGHT 894, SOUTH OF BROCKENHURST, ENGLAND

1655, 13 March, 1942

As Gloria and Byron walk around the damaged aircraft, the local farmers start showing up carrying pitch forks, shotguns, rifles, and pickaxes. The farmer on the tractor drives onto the road, stopping behind them.

Byron says, "Gloria, my friend, these folks do not look happy to see us." Coming down the road is an old car with a blue light and a sign on the roof which says 'Police'. "Here comes the official welcoming party. Why do they all look so pissed off?"

"I don't know, Byron. Helmets off."

"Shall I handle it?"

"I'll put on the charm, Byron."

The car stops abruptly and three people pile out. Two men in police uniforms and a young man in Royal Army fatigues carrying a rifle. The young soldier points the rifle at them, yelling, "Hands up, ya Krauts!"

They drop their helmets and raise their hands, and Gloria says, "Easy soldier. We're Americans. We're on your side."

"Don't try to trick me. I know these planes. They're German."

"Look at it. This is a United States Navy aircraft, son, and I'm a Navy lieutenant. Now, please put the gun down. Do I sound like a German?"

A kid with the farmers says, "It does say it's a Navy plane. It says USS Carl Vinson. USS is for America."

He looks confused, then resigned, and lowers the gun, "Since when did the Yanks let women be officers?"

"Since the Yanks finally got smart. Now, you look to be a corporal from your rank insignia. I'm Lieutenant Hoolihan and this is my flight officer, Lieutenant Standley. So, here in England what is the traditional way for a corporal to greet lieutenants?"

He snaps to attention and salutes, "My apologies, um, ma'am."

ALCONBURY RAF BASE

1657, 13 March, 1942

As Spike taxis to her hard shelter, she watches the rest of the airwing taking off and heading back to the Vinson. When she makes the turn at the end of a short taxi way, she sees a group of people near a small fenced off hill shelter. They've a large truck and a small crane. What really catches her eye is the large number of Marines guarding the compound. "Damn, Puck, what do you suppose all the Marines are guarding?"

"That is interesting, Spike. No idea. The General's booze supply?"

She reaches her hard shelter, swings the bird around to be backed in and sees Papa and a general talking. After the plane is pushed back by her ground crew, she locks the brakes, and completes the shutdown checklist. Papa and Altman walk over to her plane.

She and Puck dismount and salute, "Sir?"

Papa smiles, "Brigadier, this is Lt. Commander Samantha Hunt, commanding officer of the Black Knights, and her radar intercept officer, Lt. Hawke."

"So, this is the infamous female fighter pilot. How are you, Commander?"

Spike, "A pleasure to meet you, sir." Then turns to Papa, "Papa, we lost planes. I haven't heard from Glow Rod or Buster. Hot Pants and GQ made an emergency landing on a road."

"I heard. Are you okay?"

Fluffy walks up and salutes, "Ma'am, I got the squadron servicing aircraft. We have six birds ready to fly if need be, but right now the Tomcatters are flying CAP. I see your bird is shot the fuck up. We'll work on it. Oh, and ma'am, the berthing buildings aren't done. The Brits told Swede we had to bed everyone down with the planes. That's kinda fucked up, ma'am."

"Fluffy, is there bedding?"

"Yes, ma'am."

"Are there bath room and shower facilities?"

"Most of the hard shelters seem to have one bathroom and one shower, though not all of them are done. And, ma'am, they're as cold as hell as soon as the door opens."

"Okay, Fluffy. I need a bathroom and then I need to see Swede." They pause as a F-14 from the Tomcatters accelerates down the runway, deafening them. "Where is the squadron headquarters?"

"I ain't found it yet. At your bird, I guess."

"Okay, it will work for now. I'll be there in a second." She turns to Papa and Altman, "Sorry, Captain, General, that needed taking care of."

Papa smiles, "No problem, Commander. You can go." She leaves, walking to the head, and leaving a bemused general behind her. Papa and Puck exchange a knowing smile.

Swede sees her, but she holds up a finger and points to the head. She finishes peeing and washes her hands at the sink. Looking in the mirror she sees tired eyes and lines where there were none before. Rinsing her face, she takes a deep breath, dries off, and leaves, walking back into the hangar.

All the pilots and aircrew are waiting. Swede and Fluffy are talking to a British officer. She walks up, "Sir, I am Lt. Commander Hunt, Commander of the Black Knights," and offers a hand.

"Good day, ma'am. I'm Squadron Leader Richard Maugham at your service." He's impeccably dressed in a spotless RAF uniform and he's leaning on a cane in his left hand. "I'm your liaison officer with the Air Marshall's office. Is there any immediate needs to be serviced?"

Her southern drawl deepens, "We need to situate our people while servicing all our birds. The carrier is still nearby, and it will handle the CAP for a while, but we have very little time." Looking around the hard shelter, "Did the designers of this base consider berthing and messing arrangements?"

"They did in the buildings behind the shelters, but, unfortunately, not all is in readiness. For that, I offer my sincere apologies. I'm told the Yank Army Air Corp will be providing rations using a field expedient kitchen until all is in order."

"Needs must. Were you briefed on what our needs are? As you can see, the squadron is, well, co-ed."

"I don't follow…Ah, the women. Yes, we were told, but in truth, I did not quite believe it was so until you arrived. Quite extraordinary."

"Yes, well, we need the berthing's segregated. Males and females sleeping in the same space will be an issue. We can deal with it for now, but it will need to be addressed."

CDR 'Groovy' Miller walks up, "Spike, where is Papa?"

"He was here a bit ago. Now, I don't know. Commander Miller, this is Squadron Leader Maugham. He's our British liaison. Squadron Leader, Commander Miller, CO of the Tomcatters." The men shake hands.

Groovy says, "A pleasure, sir." Then to Spike, "I have half my squadron on CAP. You did real good up there. You were right. Most of the German planes landed in France. I'm trying to organize a strike to hit them on the ground."

She turns to Maugham, "He's right. We have a bunch of German jets scattered to hell and gone without fuel or ammo. Now is the time to hit them."

Maugham says, "We quite appreciate the strategy you adopted. We've sent several squadrons of the RAF's finest to do exactly that. It is the minister's wish to keep the American aircraft close to Britain."

"Okay, as long as we're hitting them."

Groovy, "Well, if it isn't our mission, do you want us to drop our ordinance for you guys to use? We have more on the ship."

"Groovy, yes, and thank you. Fluffy, get your boys on it, please."

"Also, I'm leaving Dirty and Moses with 303."

Papa joins them, "Thanks for giving up your ordinance, Groovy, and thank you for the men and the jet. We're going to need all we can get. Spike, what is the status of your birds?"

"We have six standing by, sir."

"Good. I want two launched in a couple of hours. Once up, I want them to sweep 50 miles south of Portsmouth, then sweep north up the English Channel using radar to make sure all is clear. While they're up, have four on ready five, and the rest on ready 15 as soon as it can be done."

"Yes, sir. Do you want to be here for the debrief?"

"Debrief is postponed. Halsey wants to be here. Are Hoolihan and Standley okay?"

"Yes, sir. They got down intact. Sir, if we have time, I want to see what is going on in that bunker." Pointing at the fenced compound with all the Marines.

HOOLIHAN AND STANDLEY

1716, 13 March, 1942

Gloria and Byron hear a faint whoop, whooping in the distance. "Corporal, what is your name, so I can write a positive remark in my report? You were doing your duty."

His chest swells, "Corporal Lance Witherspoon of the Home Guard, Baker Platoon, Charley Company, Winchester Volunteers, ma'am. My lieutenant is Barker, ma'am." Then he sees the helicopter coming in, "My Lord almighty, what is that?"

"They're here to help us. Officers, could you close the road while we sort this out?"

They nod and move out as the helicopter comes to a hover over the road and people climb out with bags of gear. ADC Gellar comes up and salutes, "Ma'am, sir, are you injured?"

"We're fine, Chief. The bird has at least one bad engine and the controls are iffy."

"Okay. We'll try to patch her up. If there are accommodations for you two here, you're better off. They are still sorting out berthing at the base."

Byron, "I'm sure they have an inn we can bill the Navy for. We'll arrange beds for you guys as well."

Gellar, "That would be cool. We'll also have to guard the bird."

The older male police officer returns and says, "I'm certain we may accommodate you in your need. May I inquire if you shot down any Jerrys?"

"Yes, sir. We shot down three."

CHAPTER 22

MESSCHERSCHMITT AIRCRAFT FACTORY, AUGSBURG, GERMANY

Hitler walks around the prototype aircraft, "It will continue to be called the ME-163, yes?"

Alexander Lippisch says, "Yes, Mein Fuhrer. With the turbojet engine, longer fuselage, landing gear, and greater fuel capacity, this Swallow will be a huge asset for our pilots. Never will bombers fly over our Fatherland."

"It is good. But can pilots fly it? The rocket plane, I understand, was difficult."

"Mein Fuhrer, that is the gift of the new engines. The fuel is vastly more stable and with the added length, it is easier to fly. We have also added flaps and slats to aid in take-off and landing. The aircraft is revolutionary."

"Good. I want them built as fast as possible. When the missiles and radar are ready, incorporate them. When will the first be ready for the Luftwaffe?"

"Yes, Mein Fuhrer. The first will be ready in no more than six months if our supplies keep up. If all goes well, perhaps five months."

"Finish them in four months. And, Herr Lippisch, design another three times as large for a bomber. Give it a range for New York and back."

"Yes, Mein Fuhrer. Heil Hitler!" He salutes.

ALCONBURY RAF BASE

1717, 13 March, 1942

Altman joins Holtz and Hunt as they walk toward the mysterious compound. When they approach, a Marine sergeant steps forward, "ID?"

They present their ID, and the Marine says, "Captain, Commander, you are on the list. Sorry, General, but you are not cleared."

"Bull shit. These two work for me. If they are cleared, I am cleared."

"I'm sorry, sir. I have my orders."

"From who? I'm the ranking American in England. I demand you let me in."

Holtz says, "General, we'll only be a moment. Let me see if I can sort this out."

Altman asks the Marine, "What would you do if I just pushed by?"

"Sir, I would shoot you. Please, don't"

Holtz and Hunt look at each other. Holtz says, "General, we'll only be a moment. Let me see if I can sort this out."

"Very well, Captain, but I want to know, in detail, what this is all about."

They walk through the check point and into the bunker. It's configured so you have to make two turns underground to get to the door. Only a direct hit would damage it. They walk into an anteroom, and beyond that is a large steel room with a large cradle, a work bench, and a desk. Standing in the entrance of the inner room is Lt. Commander Shawn Hughes, his back to the door, directing a chief and four sailors in the storage of a large bomb.

Sam, "Sir, is that what I think it is?"

Shawn spins around, startled, "Samantha! Um, Commander, Captain, yes, it is."

Holtz asks, "We're storing a nuclear device on our base? Does that mean the President has plans to use it?"

"No, sir. As I understand, it's for counter strike only. Well, unless ordered otherwise by the President." Hughes hands Holtz a packet of papers off the desk.

Holtz asks, "Who is cleared into this building?"

"Besides the tech's, only Admiral Klindt, Admiral Lee, you, Commander Hunt, Lt. Swedenborg, and myself. We are to brief Prime Minister Churchill before I leave."

Sam asks, "Who else besides us can know it is here?"

"Same list, plus Churchill. No one else. The guys who came back will probably figure it out. They need to be told it cannot be discussed, even in passing. If the Germans get wind that it's here, they will spare nothing to destroy it."

Holtz says, "We have a brigadier general outside that wants to know what's going on. Commander Hunt, I will deal with him. I take it you two know each other?"

Sam smiles, "Yes, Shawn and I were on the brain trust. This is Lieutenant Commander Shawn Hughes. Shawn, this is Captain Holtz."

Holtz nods, "A pleasure to meet you. The three of us will go over the briefing materials you have for Churchill later. I'll go disappoint the brigadier. You two stay here while I sort it out. Spike, the brigadier has his panties in a twist over the girl thing. Let me deal with him, okay?"

"Yes, sir," and she watches Holtz leave. She turns to Shawn, "How much longer do you have to be in here?"

He turns to MMC Chatman, a thin black man with intelligent eyes, "Have you performed the post transport checks of the device?"

"In progress, sir. About 10 minutes."

He turns to Sam with a little smile, "10 minutes."

"I sure didn't expect this situation."

"I know. This thing is a colossal burden. The President told Churchill that we do have a few nuclear devices and Churchill begged for one. I got sucked in because there are no nuclear weapon types as part of the brain trust crew. I understood how it has to stored and secured, so here I am."

"It's good to see you."

"Yeah, it's good to see you, too. I see you have the scarf on."

"Always. You probably didn't get my last letter."

"If you sent it recently, no. You probably haven't gotten any mail since Australia."

"Not one. It will be nice to catch up," and she grins.

Smiling, "How are you doing, Samantha?"

"Good. We've been fighting since we got here. Halsey's been pissed at me since Wake. I got into a little trouble in Australia. The Governor was a misogynist ass, and I, well, I'm me. It didn't go well."

He chuckles, "Samantha, don't stop being you. You're the you I... Don't let anyone change you. Okay?"

"Yeah, working on it."

"What happened up there? You were in a fight?"

"Yes, they're patching up my bird as we speak."

"How many kills?"

"No, Shawn, I can't."

"Okay, I think I get it."

MMC Chatman says, "We're finished, sir. The device checks out and our inventory is complete."

Hughes looks it over and signs the paperwork. "I'll be back at random times to inspect the storage and condition of the device. Do see it's always in order."

"Yes, sir. Sir, we understand what is at stake."

Hughes nods, "Carry on." He and Sam leave the bunker and they see Altman and Holtz talking. They slip away from them, walking toward her hardstand, "It's good to see you, Shawn, but I have to go debrief."

"I understand, but you know, Samantha, you can talk to me. You can't talk to your subordinates and Holtz. Well, Holtz isn't the type to have a listening ear."

"Yeah. You know, my friends call me Sam," smiles and looks up at the sky.

"Sorry, Sam it is. I'm also sorry I kinda slipped back there when you came in."

"It's fine, we're friends. It wasn't a slip. Is it lonely in Bremerton? Are you missing your family?"

"Yeah, it can be, but I have so much to do, so many hats to wear, mostly, I'm just too tired to notice. I have spent some time with my grandpa and grandma out in Idaho. I even met my dad. He's two years old."

Laughing, she touches his arm, "Oh my."

"My family has always been close, Sam. They just folded me in. Have you heard from your family yet? The Navy sent out letters."

"Yes, from my grandmother. She let me know there is plenty of work on the farm and no shortage of young men. God, it was so her...so southern woman. You know, they can be almost as bad as Jewish mothers are supposed to be. I wrote her. It will be interesting when I get a chance to visit, whenever that will be. God knows."

"Got that. Anyway, I'm doing fine. Our hovercraft venture is paying off, too. The prototype passed trials with the Navy and Marine Corps last week."

"You got that going that fast? Wow."

"Yep, there's a war on. Anyway, the Navy ordered 5000 at $20,000 each. They cost about $18,000 to make. We're already building the manufacturing and slipway infrastructure. We made the first one by hand at his yard. Now, it's getting the people to make the things. Luckily, we've been able to hire enough people for the time being. We're advertising for women to work in the yard. They're showing up. It's great." He stops, takes her arm, and turns her toward him, "Sam, that's ten million dollars. Split three ways it's, well, it's a butt load."

"Who's the third guy?"

"His name is Joe Meacham. He owns a boat yard in Port Orchard. We'd partnered 50/50, but we didn't have the capital to get the prototype built and then build the infrastructure until you came in."

"I'm glad I could help."

"You're not tracking the money, are you?"

"Not, really. That's not a priority in my life, right now."

"Look, I'm hoping that by building these boats we'll save some Marine's and soldier's lives."

"Right, good. My dad is a Marine right now. He fought at Guadalcanal. Maybe that won't happen, but he'll be fighting in the Pacific somewhere."

"I know, you said when we were in the brain trust. It seems like a million years ago. Are you okay, Sam?"

She lowers her head, then looks up, "Shawn, I…I don't know what okay is."

"You have to talk to someone. Talk to me. I'll never betray your trust. I can feel you carrying this huge weight. Let me carry some of it for you."

"I don't think it works that way, Shawn. You just can't take someone else's…someone else's guilt."

"The killing. Is that it?"

"Yeah, that's it. I...Shawn, what kind of terrible person am I? It doesn't hit me up there. It's get it done or die. And, I have to take care of my guys. I know it has to be done. I know the stakes of this war. Especially this war. But, it's still hard. I probably just took the lives of ten people, maybe more."

He takes her hands, and gazes into her eyes, "Sam, you're not a terrible person. You're an amazing person called on to do a terrible duty. You know, I could spout some rah-rah crap, but it would all be bullshit. I've never done what you do. I can't say I really understand it, viscerally. I promise I will do my very best to understand and I will never judge you for what you share."

"Shawn, how can you not judge me? Everybody seems to be measuring me. Halsey is pissed off at me for something I said to the CAG. Something he was never supposed to hear. I've so screwed up as a leader, I didn't even get a fucking Navy Achievement Medal. Nobody wants me in the sky, except for Lee. For him, I'm some kind of bragging rights." She takes a deep breath and pulls her hands away, "Shawn, I'm a mess and you are better off not even knowing me."

He takes a deep breath, fighting the anger rising in him, "Sam, I do know you. I just said I'm here for you. I don't give a flying fuck what anyone else thinks. Admiral Halsey is an idiot if he is mad at you. I'd wager whatever you said, it was the truth."

Sam starts laughing, "Damn it, Shawn, you always go straight to the jugular. It was right after we lost Wake. I stomped into Holtz's office mad. Oh, was I mad. I asked what idiot focused on the Japanese carriers instead of the invasion beaches. All I could think of was those Marines down there so desperately needing our help. Instead of helping them, we blew up some carriers, that in the greater scheme of things, don't really matter anymore. Especially, now that the Vinson is here. Admiral Halsey was standing behind me in the door."

"Damn, and double damn. He shouldn't have done that," gently touching her hand. "You were right. But, you know, people hate hearing they've done wrong, especially when, deep down, they know they've screwed up. And when some subordinate points it out, well, oh boy, that's a problem. Anyway, you are right. The loss of Wake was a disaster. You haven't got any medals? Anything?"

"I got the unit medals, the Air Medal, and Gloria and I got the lifesaving medal for SAR swimming during the sinking of the Stoddert. I was awarded the Distinguished Flying Cross for over ten kills, like everyone else. Any other unit commander in my position would have received at least a Meritorious Service Medal for what I've done. And that is what is getting to me. It's so hard. I know I'm not supposed to care, but I do. It's like I don't matter. Now, we're being cast away from the carrier. Why us? The Tomcatters have as many functional birds and their commander is more experienced."

"I can actually answer that last one. Churchill specifically requested our most effective squadron. That's yours. Your squadron shot down 178 Japanese aircraft. The next closest is the Tomcatters at 102. I talked to Admiral Lee about it on our way out here. He was in the phone conference with Churchill and Roosevelt. You are not being punished. And, Sam, I don't think you're just bragging rights with Lee. He's really proud of you, yes. He thinks the world of you. The medal thing, that is something else. I'll talk to Lee about it."

"No, Shawn, no. Please, don't. If anyone knew I was whining about not getting medals, I would look…Shawn, it isn't the point. I don't care about the medals. It's just what the lack of medals means. They do not trust me in command."

"I'm sorry. I said I would listen, and there I go trying to fix it. Sorry. Sam, Lee trusts you. Klindt trusts you." He pauses as an F-14 accelerates down the runway.

Holtz walk out of one of the hard shelters, spots her and points to the end of the runway where a C-2 Greyhound is on final.

"Shawn, I got to go. When do you leave?"

"When I'm convinced that the item is secured and Churchill is briefed."

"Okay, maybe dinner. I'll see you later." She touches his hand and walks toward Papa and a group of people waiting for the plane to stop. She realizes she feels better.

Just talking with Shawn helped, a lot. She smiles as she joins Papa, Swede, the other officers of the squadron, and Fluffy.

Papa turns to her, "Spike, Halsey is coming in for a debrief. Do we have a place?"

She turns to Swede and he says, "Yes, sir, ma'am. One half of the command building is a ready room."

CHAPTER 23

US NAVY READY ROOM, RAF, ALCONBURY

1820, 13 March, 1942

The debrief takes place in a long narrow room, furnished as a classroom, at the north end of the command building, behind the hard shelters. Halsey, Holtz, Maugham and Swede are in the first row. Sam finishes up the debrief, "So, we broke the attack on the Vinson and she is back at sea. We've lost one, maybe two aircraft, depending on the damage to Hoolihan's bird. We've also gained an F/A-18 and a bird from the Tomcatters. Lieutenant Cash, if we can patch you up in time, we'll send you back to the Vinson.

"The Knights shot down about forty aircraft in two engagements. Once gun camera footage is available, we'll have better numbers. We know they have about one hundred and twenty, so we're still facing at least eighty aircraft. We have a helo on site with a repair crew for Hoolihan's bird. That's about it. Captain, do you have anything to add?"

Holtz walks to the front, "All of you did very well. Lieutenant Klint, Lieutenant Moscowitz, and Lieutenant Cash, we've shipped all your sea bags here. All of you are now assigned to the Black Knights. I just got word on your plane, Lieutenant Cash. Given the condition of your F/A-18, it isn't going to catch the boat. Our ability to fix it is also limited. Lieutenant, can you transition to the '14?"

Cash smiles, "Yes, sir."

"Good, we'll sort out the flight rotations later. Admiral Halsey, the floor is yours."

Halsey walks to the front and surveys the room. The aircrew in front of him look like hell. They're tired and dirty, but as he meets their eyes, he sees a difference from when he first met them only a few months ago. "I know last December you left on a peace time cruise. You are now veterans of six air battles. In the beginning you wondered how well you would handle combat. Now, there is no doubt. Each of you is a hardened warrior.

"Today, you faced the Germans twice. In the first engagement, you slapped them good and sent them packing. In the second, you wiped out a third of their force." He pauses, "I know you lost friends today, and it is right to mourn them. But, today, the odds were 25 to one. I have never heard of a more lop-sided victory since the Battle of Salamis. And you were handicapped going into it, because you were blind.

"You're commanding officer, Commander Hunt, devised a brilliant plan to use every available asset. Her plan to hit them as they retreated, forcing them to expend more fuel, was outstanding. As the Gold Eagle leaves you, I know Britain is in good hands. I am proud of you all. Get some rest. Captain Holtz, Commander Hunt, could I have a word?"

Sam stands, stunned at Halsey's words. As the aircrew file out, she follows him and Holtz to a conference room. As they walk, YN1 Cooper, her yeoman intercepts them and hands Sam a paper bag and a thermos. He just says, "Eat, ma'am," and walks away.

In Holtz's conference room Halsey says, "Your yeoman is right. You have to be starving. Eat." She pulls out a sandwich and starts in as Halsey continues, "Commander Hunt, you did very well. Now, we are estimating that they have at least eighty aircraft left of the those that came back. They'll want to conserve them until they can get their production of new planes up and running. They will not fall for the same trick twice. The goal, of course, is to protect Britain, but to do that you'll need to preserve your force.

"I am told that new replacement jets are still six to nine months away. You must survive. Even if you lose a battle or two, you must survive. Admiral Nimitz once famously said he was the only man who could lose the war in a day. Really, that applies to you two, as well. You must survive. I can't give you more planes than you already have, and we split the parts down the line. Can you think of anything else you need?"

Sam asks, "Sir, do we have operating funds?"

Holtz answers, "They gave us one and half million dollars. We're fine for now."

Halsey asks Holtz, "You understand your role?"

"Yes, but why did they pick 'Commander United States Naval Forces Britain'?"

"I'm told an American submarine, the USS San Francisco, will be arriving in Scotland in the next month or so. You are in charge of that, as well."

"Oh, that explains the Mark-48 torpedoes we got. Thank you, sir."

"Thank you, Captain, Commander." Looking them in the eyes, "Proceed. You know what to do."

Halsey rises, turns and leaves. Holtz turns his head and looks at Sam, eyebrows raised, then nods his head. "Right." Then he goes, following Halsey.

She sits, thinking, and absentmindedly finishes two roast beef sandwiches, an apple, an orange, and the thermos of coffee. Then she walks out of the building, heading for her hard shelter. She desperately needs a shower and some sleep.

The sun is setting, turning the sky shades of red, orange, and gold. She watches the Greyhound carrying Halsey back to the carrier, escorted by the last two Tomcatters, take off. They fly into the setting sun, soon lost to sight in the glowing rays. The realization hits her, they are now alone.

Lowering her eyes, she sees Shawn walking toward her. Their gazes meet and Sam smiles.

THE END

NOTES

When starting a novel of this type it is necessary to decide at the outset how to tackle a number of issues. The Navy uses a great deal of jargon, technical terms, and acronyms that are used in speech. Eliminating this techno-speak from dialog would remove the character of the whole story. We also recognize that leaving the jargon in could be confusing to readers not familiar with the military. It was decided to include a glossary and leave the language as it would be spoken with a few exceptions. When ships communicate over radio each ship has a code name that is used in place of the actual ship's name. As this would be confusing, we opted to use the ship's name. Many complex procedures are simplified to keep the story flowing and reduce confusion. Aircraft numbers are generally based on the bureau (serial) number of the plane regardless who the pilot is. The exception is the commanding officer whose number is always one. Though this may be confusing generally the reader should be able to follow the dialog without the number cue. Where events are occurring simultaneously, yet in different time zones the author chose to adopt Greenwich Mean Time for clarity. In all other sections, local time is used. A number of other technical details were changed to prevent revealing classified information.

A note on naval rank structure. In other services an enlisted person is addressed by rank, "Corporal, Sargent," etc. In the Navy sailors are addressed with rate and rank. An E-6 is not normally addressed as, "Petty Officer First Class." He or she is addressed as, "MM1, BT1, BM1" etc. The rate is the job classification of the sailor, be that machinist mate (engine room equipment operator), or mess specialist (cook). A more comprehensive list of rates can be found in the glossary or on line. The rank of enlisted sailors is in three groups of three ranks. E-1 through E-3 sailors are non-petty officers. These are new sailors who may or may not yet have a rate. E-4 through E-6 sailors are petty officers. These sailors are the technical experts and watch-standers who keep the navy running. E-4's are third class, E-5's are second class, and E-6 are first class petty officers. E-7 through E-9 sailors are middle managers. They are Chief, Senior Chief, and Master Chief. Chiefs are system experts who train, lead and guide instead of operating equipment. The colloquial for E-7 is, "Chief." For E-8's it is, "Senior." No one calls a Master Chief, "Master." Calling a senior or master chief, "Chief," is not an insult. There are essentially two types of officer. Line officers can command vessels and aircraft. Non-line, or limited duty officers are doctors, dentists, chaplains, civil engineer corps, or have other specific duties.

Glossary

16: VHF channel 16 is the international emergency channel. It is also, generally the channel used to communicate in the open, or non-encrypted communications.

1MC: General announcing system. Ship wide loud speaker system.

2nd Lt.: Second Lieutenant. Army and USMC rank. (O-1)

(Number)K: Fuel state. K for thousand pounds.

AA: Navy rank. Airman Apprentice (E-2).

AB: Navy enlisted rate. Aviation Boatswain's Mate. They do many duties on the flight and hanger decks and maintain other aviation equipment. ABAA through ABMC.

AD: Naval aviation rating. Aviation Machinist. ADAA through ADCM. AD's maintain aircraft structural components, flight surfaces, and engines.

ADM: Admiral. Naval Officer rank (O-10). Also used colloquially for Rear Admirals Lower and Upper, and Vice Admirals (O-7 through 9).

AE: Navy rate. Aviation Electrician. They maintain the electrical generation, conversion and distribution systems associated with jet aircraft. AEA through AECM

AGL: Above Ground Level.

Ahead (Bell): The standard bells, or speeds of a ship are ahead 1/3, ahead 2/3, ahead Standard, Ahead full, and Ahead Flank. The number is the amount of revolutions per minute of the shaft.

Ahead Flank Emergency: Order to come to the fastest ahead speed as fast as possible. See Bell.

Air Boss: The ship's force air department head. The air boss commands all operations on the flight deck and hanger deck.

Air Chief Marshall: Royal Air Force Officer rank. Equivalent to Vice Admiral or Lieutenant General.

Air Commodore: Royal Air Force Officer rank. Equivalent to Captain or Colonel.

Air Marshall: Royal Air Force Officer rank. Equivalent to Rear Admiral or the current Rear Adm Upper Half or Major General.

Air Vice-Marshall: Royal Air Force Officer rank. Equivalent to Commodore or the current Rear Adm Lower Half or Brigadier General.

Amphenol: Multi-prong electronic or electrical connection.

AN: Naval Enlisted non-designated aviation rank. Airman (E-3).

AO: Enlisted rate. Aviation Ordinanceman. AOAA through AOCM. They inspect, care for and handle air delivered ordinance.

Arco: When an aircraft flies as a refueler they are given a special call sign. Usually the name of a gas station chain.

ASROC: Anti-submarine rocket. A torpedo delivered by a rocket.

ASW: Anti-submarine warfare.

AT: Navy rate. Aviation Electronics Technician. They maintain the complex electronic equipment associated with jet aircraft. ATA through ATCM

Auto-gyro: An emergency landing technique that uses the wind blowing through the helicopter rotors to keep them spinning, then uses the collective to slow the bird's descent at the last moment.

(AW): Naval specialist Badge. Air Warfare Specialist. Placed after rate such as AD1(AW).

Back (Bell): Astern bells for a marine engine. Back 1/3, Back 2/3, and Back Full.

Back Full Emergency: Astern bell to be answered as fast as possible.

Bandit: NATO code for enemy aircraft.

Battalion: Army/USMC tactical unit smaller than a brigade or regiment but larger than a company. Smallest unit designed to function independently. Generally commanded by a LT Colonel.

BDU: Battle Dress, Utility. The basic Army and Marine uniform.

Bell: The speed a ship is traveling at: Ahead they are Ahead 1/3, Ahead 2/3, Ahead Standard, Ahead Full, and Ahead Flank. Astern they are Back 1/3, Back 2/3, and Back full. In an emergency the order given is ahead flank emergency, or back full emergency which is a command to go as fast as possible.

Bearing: Compass or relative bearing in degrees from 0 to 360. Compass is true north, not magnetic north. Relative bearing puts 000 as straight in front of the bow of the ship and clocks degrees clockwise around the ship.

Bingo Fuel: Near the minimum to safely return to base.

Binnacle List: List of people sick or injured. Every unit and division maintains the Binnacle List and turns it in daily.

Blow: Submarines use ballast tanks to surface or submerge. By blowing high pressure air into the tanks water can be displaced and the vessel surfaces.

Blue Tails: Nick name for the VAW-122 Griffins. VAW-122 flies the E-2C Hawkeye radar plane.

Blue Water Ops: Carrier operations beyond reach of alternative air fields. You land on the carrier or swim.

Boatswain's Mate of the Watch (BMOW): In charge of all the lookouts, the helm and lee helm. The BMOW pipes (whistles) required ships announcements.

Bogey: An unidentified aircraft.

Boiler: Boilers generate the steam for propulsion, electrical generation, water distillation, and other uses.

Bolter: An aircraft missing the arresting wire.

Bridge: The ship's navigational control center. Where we drive the ship. The Officer of the Deck (OOD) is in charge except when the CO or XO are present. The Conning Officer directs the ship's coarse and speed. The Boatswains Mate of the Watch (BMOW), Quartermaster of the Watch (QMOW), Helm and Lee Helm are stationed here.

Brigade: Army/ Marine Tactical unit smaller than a Division and larger than a Battalion. Sometimes called a Regiment. Generally commanded by a Colonel or Brigadier General. They are usually armor, infantry, or airborne focused for the Army but still contain other units to permit independent operations.

BTOW: Boiler Technician of the watch. Senior watch in a boiler room.

BT: Navy Enlisted rate. Boiler Technician. BTFA through BTCM. Currently the BT rate is merged with the MM rate. Boiler Technicians operate and maintain marine boilers.

CAG: Commander Air Group. The CAG is in charge of all the air squadrons attached to the ship. The CAG is the counterpart to the ship's commanding officer. The carrier CO is always the senior.

Call the Ball: The Landing Signal Officer asks the pilot if they can see the Fresnel lens that shows the correct glide slope for landing.

Control: In a submarine Control is a room and watch station equivalent to both the bridge and combat control center on a surface ship.

Calico: NATO brevity code for an intruder on the radio net.

CAP: Combat Air Patrol. A fighter mission to circle an area ready to defend the fleet.

CAPT: Captain: Army and USMC rank. (O-3)

CAPT: Captain: Naval Officer rank (O-6).

CATCC: Carrier Air Traffic Control Center. This center controls all aircraft within 50 miles of the ship and manages take offs and landings.

CAV or Cavalry: Specialized Army Unit: These are units historically used for reconnaissance for larger units. They can be Armor, Airmobile, or Airborne. By WW2 the CAV distinctions were somewhat less then in wars past. Today the distinction is more historical than practical.

CDR: Naval Officer rank. Commander (O-5).

CHENG: Chief Engineer. Engineering department head.

CMAA: Chief Master at arms. A senior cop on a Navy ship.

COL: Army and USMC rank. (O-6)

Combat: Sometimes Combat control center. Weapon's and communications control center on a naval ship. The CO generally goes to combat during battle stations (General Quarters).

Combat Engineer: Specialized Army or USMC person who is trained to support combat operations by destroying obstacles. Structural engineers build things. Combat engineers blow them up.

Commodore: USN Officer rank. Equivalent to current Rear Admiral Lower half or Brigadier General. This rank was reauthorized in 1942 and discontinued after the war. It has been brought back, changed, and discarded since for the rank Rear Admiral Lower Half. If a unit of ships does not have an Admiral in charge the senior or assigned Captain can take the title Commodore to designate they are in charge of the group. This does not involve any change of pay or rank.

Company: Army/Marine tactical unit. Generally Commanded by a Captain. They are made up of a number of platoons and are organized into Battalions. Generally, companies are too small to function independently.

CORPS: Army tactical unit. Normally commanded by a Lieutenant General or General. It is a group of divisions and/or other units. Corps are not permanently assigned their divisions but rather receive and lose units based on need.

COTAC: Copilot Tactical Coordinator. Antisubmarine duty on S-3 Viking Aircraft.

Decimal: On radio the word 'Decimal' is used to indicate tenths. Thus fuel at 9 decimal 2 is 9,200 pounds. Fuel is always given as weight.

Diesel Dyke: Nickname for women in the engineering fields, regardless of their rating. Obviously, it is not a term of respect and isn't tolerated in the modern Navy.

Division (Army/ USMC): Army and Marine Corps organizational unit. Army/USMC Divisions are tactical units commanded by a Brigadier or Lieutenant General that command a number of Brigades and supporting units. They are sometimes armor, infantry, airborne specific but contain all those other units needed to be an independent military unit.

Division (Navy): Naval organizational unit. Naval units are divided into Departments and Divisions. Divisions are functionally oriented units with all the enlisted members typically of one rating.

Eject: Order to initiate the ejection sequence for abandoning a doomed aircraft. Once ordered everyone must eject.

Electric Boat: Submarine Manufacturing firm based in Groton and other New England towns. In 1952 it merged with General Dynamics. Most US submarines are made by Electric Boat.

ELT: Navy Enlisted trade. Some MM's are qualified Engineering Laboratory Technician (Nuclear). They are chemistry and radiation specialists, though they also stand normal mechanical watches.

EM: Navy Enlisted rate. Electrician's Mate. Electricians operate the electrical distribution system on the ship, and also maintain all the electrical equipment. EMFN through EMCM.

EMP: Electro-Magnetic Pulse. A powerful change in the magnetic field. An EMP could damage or destroy electronic and electric gear.

Engine Room: Space where the main engines, electrical generators, and water distilling unit are located. This equipment is operated and maintained by Machinist Mates.

ENS: Ensign: Naval Officer rank (O-1). Junior most officer. Sometimes called a butter bar for their rank insignia which is a single gold bar.

EOOW: Engineering Officer Of the Watch. Watch stander in charge of the propulsion plant. Normally a Lt. on a nuclear ship. Sometimes a senior or master chief on conventional powered ships.

ETA: Estimated Time of Arrival.

F-14: The Tomcat. An all-weather interceptor and fleet defense fighter.

Faking hose: Laying out a hose or line in parallel lines so the hose can be safely charged or the line let go without jamming.

Far CAP: Combat Air Patrol. Far CAP is a defensive position away from the fleet.

Fire room: Location of the boilers in a fossil fueled steam ship.

Fire Team: An Army and USMC tactical unit consisting of two to four people and generally commanded by a Corporal. A squad will typically have two to four fire teams.

Flight Lieutenant: Royal Air Force Officer rank. Equivalent to Lieutenant Junior Grade (Navy) or Lieutenant (Army, USMC).

Flight Sergeant: RAF senior enlisted rank. Equivalent to Master Sergeant. May or may not be air crew.

Flying Officer: Royal Air Force Officer rank. Equivalent to Ensign or Second Lieutenant.

FN: Navy Enlisted rank. Fireman (E-3). A non-designated engineering striker. If designated his rate would precede his rank.

FOD Walk Down: Walking the flight deck looking for FOD (Foreign Object Damage) that could damage aircraft.

Fox (number): Part of NATO brevity code. It is a call announcing the firing of a missile. The number designates the type of missile. 1 is short to intermediate range radar guided missile. 2 is a short range heat seeking missile. 3 is a long range radar guided missile.

Fuel state: How much fuel you have on board in thousands of pounds. (10 decimal 1 = 10,100lbs.)

'G's: Gravities. One 'G' is equal to normal earth gravity. Two is twice earth gravity etc.

General Quarters: The call to man battle stations and prepare the vessel to fight.

Gertrude: Nick name for a short range underwater phone.

GMG: Navy Enlisted rate. Gunners Mate Guns. Gunner's Mates operate and maintain the weapons on a ship. The rate is split between Gunner's Mate Guns (GMG) and Gunner's Mate Missiles (GMM). GMGSA through GMGMC.

GMM: Navy Enlisted rate. Gunners Mate Missiles. Gunner's Mates operate and maintain the weapons on a ship. The rate is split between Gunner's Mate Guns (GMG) and Gunner's Mate Missiles (GMM). GMMSA through GMMMC.

Gold Eagle: Official nickname of the Carl Vinson. Every Navy ship is given an official nickname. The crews often give an unofficial nickname. In our novel series we sometimes use these as radio call signs. That would not normally be true ship to ship, but often used in air operations.

Group Captain: Royal Air Force Officer rank. Commander or Lieutenant Colonel.

GySGT: Gunnery Sergeant. USMC enlisted rank. (E-7) Generally an assistant Company commander or assistant to a higher rank officer or enlisted. As an assistant company commander, they are responsible for training the company commander and all servicemen under them. It is a critical and important job.

HT: Navy Enlisted rate. Hull Technician. HT's are Damage control and repair experts. They also operate the sewer system on the ship earning them the undesirable nickname "turd chaser". HTFA through HTMC.

HY-80: Hardened steel used for special applications by the Navy. 3/8" will stop most rifle bullets.

ILS: Instrument Landing system. An aircraft system that helps pilots line up with a runway they cannot see.

Khaki: Navy slang term for chiefs and officers because they wear khaki colored uniforms.

Knight (number): Call sign of fighters flying for VFW-154, the Black Knights.

Landing Signal Officer: A pilot positioned near the rear of the carrier to help guide pilots in. The LSO also grades landings.

Law of Continuity of Suckage: Submarine phrase. Once the hatch is shut suckage can neither be created or destroyed. Meaning when one person gets a good deal another gets screwed. This is what happens when you lock a bunch of nukes in a tube for months on end.

Laze: Use a laser to designate where ordinance is to drop.

LCDR: Naval Officer rank. Lieutenant Commander (O-4).

LPO: Naval enlisted position. Leading Petty Officer is the "Foreman" for a division. Usually an E-6.

Lt: Army and USMC rank. (O-2) Lieutenants are generally platoon officers or assistants to the commander of a larger unit.

Lt.: Naval officer rank. Lieutenant (O-3). Generally, a Division Officer in smaller units a lieutenant might be the XO or even CO.

Lt. COL: Army and USMC rank. (O-5) Generally commands a Battalion sized unit or serves as an assistant to the commander of a larger unit.

Lt. JG: Naval Officer rank. Lieutenant Junior Grade. (O-2.) Generally a division officer or assistant to a more senior officer.

MA: Navy Enlisted rate. Master at Arms. Similar to Military police MA's enforce uniform and behavior rules. As such they are generally disliked. MA3 through MACM.

Magic (number): Call sign for an EA-6B Prowler, radar jamming aircraft of VAQ-133 Wizards.

MAJ: Major: Army and USMC rank. (O-4) Majors are sometimes company commanders but more often serve as assistants to higher rank officers. In the Pentagon you can't throw a stick without hitting a Major.

Marshall of the RAF: Royal Air Force Officer rank. The senior officer of the service. Equivalent to Chief of Naval Operations or Army Chief of Staff.

Master Chief: Naval Enlisted Rank (E-9).

Mini Boss: The air boss's assistant. They divide the observation duties in PRIFLY.

MM: Navy Enlisted rate. Machinist's Mate. They operate and maintain the machinery associated with ship's propulsion, auxiliary gear, and nuclear power systems. MMFA through MMCM. All nukes leave A school as MM3.

MMOW: Machinist's Mate Of the Watch. Senior watch stander in an engine room. Sometimes called the Engine Room Supervisor. It is a watch station and not a rank.

MOS: Military Occupational Specialty. It is what a soldier or marine is trained to do. Be that infantry, armor, special forces, supply, radio operator, combat engineer or a myriad of other jobs. Generally, it is not used in the way ones rate is in the navy. You don't call a sergeant in the infantry an infantry sergeant. There are some positional title changes for those in special units such as cavalry.

NAM: Navy Achievement Medal. A medal for individual meritorious accomplishment. When a V device is added for valor it signifies the award was for combat actions.

NAVSEA 08: Designation for the leader of the U. S. Navy Nuclear Power Program.

Navy Expeditionary Medal: Medal issued for service in a combat zone designated by congress.

NOE: Nap of earth. Order to fly as low as safely possible.

NTDS: Naval Tactical Data System. A system that shares sensor data with other ships.

Nuke: Nickname for anyone in the nuclear power career field. It is sometime used derisively. It is even said "Fuckingnuke" is one word.

Nuclear waste: Nickname for anyone who fails to complete nuclear training or is otherwise removed from the program. It is generally used with respect by nukes.

MW: Megawatt. One million watts. 1,000,000 watts. Most nuclear power plants are measured in MW.

O-2 Plant: The oxygen generation plant which removes atmospheric oxygen and compresses it into liquid oxygen used by medical and as pilot breathing air.

Officer Of the Deck (OOD): In charge of the operation and navigation of the ship underway. In port the OOD is in charge of the ship's duty section and all operations during their watch.

Op-tempo: Rate of operations over time.

OPPE: Operational Propulsion Plant Exam. Same as ORSE for conventionally powered vessels.

ORSE: Operational Reactor Safeguards Exam. Scheduled examination of propulsion plant material condition and operational compliance. A poor grade on ORSE causes career ventilation. It can be a negative mark on every nuke on board.

Passageway: Navy speak for a hallway.

Petty Officer: Colloquial phrase for an E-4 through E-6. Generally, it is only used by officers or master at arms who are about to correct the Petty Officer's behavior. Instead a sailor will address the Petty Officer with there rate. MM1 instead of PO1.

PFC: Private First Class. (E-3) Army and USMC rank.

Phoenix: AIM-54 Long range air to air missile. The F-14 was designed to carry and fire this missile. In reality the USN never actually fired one at an enemy aircraft.

Platoon: Army and USMC tactical unit consisting of two to four squads. With armor this is three to four tanks. Platoons are generally commanded by a Lieutenant or Second Lieutenant and have a Staff Sergeant, called a platoon sergeant, to train the officer and men.

PQS: Personal Qualification Standard. PQS is the system used by the Navy to qualify sailors to do their jobs.

Propulsion plant drills: Engineering operator training practicing possible casualties and problems. Continuous training is the reality of most sailors. This is to prepare operators for problems that only occur very rarely but have huge consequences if the watch team does not know what they are doing.

PRYFLY: Primary Flight Control. The highest deck in the island structure where all flight deck operations are managed.

QAO: Quality Assurance Officer. The QAO manages inspection paperwork from repairs and also personally inspects critical repairs. No system, or aircraft can be used as designed until the QAO has approved the work.

Quartermaster of the Watch (QMOW): In charge of providing navigational information to the OOD and Conning Officer. The QMOW is required to keep the ship's position updated on paper and electronic charts.

Rainbow side boys: The traditional side boys for a senior visitor, only wearing the various flight deck colored jerseys.

Reactor Auxiliary Room (RAR): The RAR is the space where the reactor support and monitoring equipment is located. It shares most of the same functions that a fire room in a conventional vessel would have. Generally, the Naval Reactor is in a separate room inside this room.

Rear Admiral Lower Half: Naval Officer rank. One Star Admiral (O-7). See Commodore for WW2 usage.

Rear Admiral Upper Half: Naval Officer rank. Two Star Admiral (O-8). Called Rear Admiral in WW2.

RIM-7: Rail launched intermediate range air to air missile. Sea Sparrow.

RIO: Radar Intercept Officer. The RIO operates the radar and weapons system in the back seat of the F-14. They are a critical half of the in flight team for fighting the aircraft.

RM: Navy enlisted rate. Radioman. They operate the radio communications gear for the Navy. They are, generally the most secretive because they are forbidden to share anything of what they see and hear.

Roger Ball (Number): Roger ball means the pilot can see the Fresnel lens glide slope indicator. The number is the total weight of the aircraft in thousands of pounds.

RTB: Return to Base.

SAM: Surface to Air Missile.

SAR: Search and Rescue.

SFC: Sergeant First Class. Army rank. (E-7) Generally an assistant company commander or assistant to a higher rank officer or enlisted. As an assistant company commander, they are responsible for training the company commander and all servicemen under them. It is a critical and important job.

SGT: Sergeant. (E-5). Army and USMC Rank. A sergeant generally is in charge of a tank, squad, or fire team. That or they serve as the assistant to more senior enlisted or officers. They are the back bone of any service.

SGT MAJ: Army and USMC enlisted rank. (E-9) Sergeant Major is the senior enlisted rank. They generally serve as senior instructors and advisors to major commands. They may have a staff under them.

SIS: British Secret Intelligence Service. Now called MI6.

SLQ-32: Called the "slick 32" it is a multi-function radar jammer carried on USN ships.

Snap 2: Early supply computer.

SOB: Son Of a Bitch. Even cuss words have acronyms.

SSGT: Staff sergeant. (E-6) Army and USMC Rank. A staff sergeant is generally an assistant platoon leader or assistant to a higher ranked person. In the role of platoon sergeant they are responsible for training the platoon officer in how to be an effective leader while also training all their subordinate servicemen. It is a vital position.

Start the Music: NATO Code phrase for commencing jamming.

Squad: Army and USMC tactical unit. Generally made up of two to four fire teams and commanded by a Sergeant. In Armor this is typically one track or vehicle.

Squadron Leader: Royal Air Force Officer rank. Equivalent to Lieutenant or Captain.

Squawked: Identification, friend or foe (IFF) Code signal.

ST: Navy Enlisted rate. Sonar Technician. Responsible for operating sonar systems on ships and submarines. STSA through STMC.

Switch Gear Room: Space where the electrical distribution system is operated. EM's stand watch in Switch Gear.

TACAN: Radio beacon aircraft use to find the carrier.

TARPS: Tactical Airborne Reconnaissance Pod System. A camera system mounted on a hard point and controlled by the RIO.

TG: Turbine Generator. An electrical Generator powered by steam.

TG/DU: Turbine Generator and Distilling Unit watch. An Engine room watch stood by an MM.

Thwarts ship passageway: A hall way aligned from side to side rather than forward and aft.

TLD: Thermal Luminescent Dosimetry. A radiation measuring device to monitor crew exposure. The nukes sometimes call it "the little dicky."

VHF: Very High Frequency. A line of sight radio.

Vice Admiral: Naval Officer rank. VADM (O-9).

Wave off: Order to abort a landing and go around.

Wing Commander: Royal Air Force Officer rank. Equivalent to Lieutenant Commander or Major.

Yankee Search: Active sonar search.

YN: Naval Enlisted rate. Yeoman. Yeomen are the administrative grease that lubricates the functioning of the Navy machine. When an officer has a good yeoman, they guard him or her jealously. It is an unofficial sport to poach one's yeoman. YNSA through YNMC.

XO: Executive officer. Second in charge of a vessel or unit. Actual rank varies based on the size of the unit. A patrol craft or air squadron XO could be a Lieutenant. On a super carrier the XO is generally a Captain.

X-Ray: Material condition X-Ray. Lowest level of water tight integrity. Only set during a work day in port.

Yoke: Material condition Yoke. Middle level of water tight integrity between X-ray (in port on work day) and Zebra (Battle Stations). At sea yoke is checked at least daily.

Zebra: Material condition Zebra. Highest level of water tight integrity.

MM1 Maki is a U.S. Navy veteran with twenty years of active service. A nuclear field machinist mate who served on the USS Carl Vinson, CVN-70, and two cruisers. During twelve years of sea time, MM1 Maki circumnavigated the earth once, transited the Panama Canal three times, served on the USS Carl Vinson during Enduring Freedom, and earned multiple campaign awards. S.R. Maki has a background in criminal justice and accounting.

See us at TheFightingTomcats.com

Email us at RoseHillPress17@gmail.com

Made in the USA
Coppell, TX
31 May 2020